T0062882

# TOUCH
# &
# TELL

# TOUCH
# &
# TELL

## A Novel by

## Samantha Harrington

### Edited by Adele Brunner

PARTRIDGE

**To order additional copies of this book, contact**
Toll Free 800 101 2657 (Singapore)
Toll Free 1 800 81 7340 (Malaysia)
orders.singapore@partridgepublishing.com

www.partridgepublishing.com/singapore

For M.J.R, my Hero.

# Chapter 1

Darkness
Wading through fog thick as glue
In a body made of lead
Darkness


Muted light filters through
Muffled sounds
Heaviness weighs like a blanket of stone, pulling me down
Darkness envelops me


Lighter
Closer to the surface
Indistinct voices
Heaviness, dragging me under

Darkness

Clawing my way up to the light
Voices
Words
"Juno? Juno? It's me darling. Can you hear me?"
Yes, yes! I can hear you, I want to answer but the words won't come.
I try to open my eyes but the effort is too much for me.
It is enough to know he is here with me.
I surrender to the heaviness, diving back down into the
Darkness

# Chapter 2

My eyes are open but everything is blurred. The room is dimly lit. My vision slowly clears as I blink several times and look around. I am in a bed. It is not mine. I am not alone. There are other beds. There are people in them. Everyone appears to be sleeping. Other than muted beeping, everything is quiet. It seems to be night and I suddenly realise I am in hospital. I have no idea why. My heart starts racing, as does my mind. What's happened? What's going on?

I try to sit up. I manage to lift my head and shoulders before the effort becomes too much. Both my wrists are taped and have cords coming out of them. I am hooked to a drip. The bag hanging from its stand is half full with clear fluid. A plastic tube runs from the bag and is connected to a tiny needle taped to the back of my hand. On the left is a monitor. Its glowing blue numbers seem to change often but mean nothing to me. A cord leads from the machine to a clip with a red glowing light at its tip. It's clasped to the index finger of my left hand. Those figures on the monitor are mine.

I try to call out but a pathetic mewl is all that escapes. My mouth is dry. My tongue feels like a swollen dead weight. The monitor I am attached to seems to reflect my rising panic. In the centre of the room a nurse, previously hidden from view, rises from behind a circular workstation. She walks quickly and soundlessly over to my bed. She has a kind face and smiles warmly. She speaks to me softly, all the while checking and making adjustments to the equipment I am attached to.

"Juno, welcome back!"

Where have I been? I wonder. Before I can make another attempt at speech she goes on.

"I am just going to call the doctor to let him know you're awake and I will be right back with you, ok?"

I nod or at least I try to. This seems to work: still smiling, she retraces her steps to the centre of the room. My heart is still working overtime, but the terror has subsided a little.

She leans over the top of the counter to pick up a phone, pressing buttons on the handset before holding it to her ear. I hear her speaking faintly but cannot make out the words. She mentioned calling a doctor. I thoroughly scan my body. There are no bandages anywhere visible, only tape on my hands where I am hooked up to machines. I alternately wiggle both my legs and carefully watch the bed covers as they move. I feel totally depleted but am in no pain. I seem to be physically fine. I try to think, to remember, but what am I supposed to be remembering? If I am not hurt, why am I in hospital? Why do I need a doctor?

The smiling nurse makes her way back to me and once again I attempt to find my voice.

"Why am I here?"

What comes out is croaky and barely above a whisper, but in this eerily quiet room it's enough to be heard.

"Both your father and Dr. Davis are on their way and will be able to answer all your questions. How are you feeling?"

Answering questions with questions is one of my mum's favourite ways of diverting my attention. I am determined not to be distracted now.

"Tired but fine, I guess. I'm just very confused. I have no idea why I'm here. Am I sick?"

Watching her face closely, I realise she is considering what to say and probably, more importantly, what not to say. Finally, she opens her mouth to speak. At that exact moment, a machine across the room begins to beep.

She looks apologetic but there's more than a hint of relief in her eyes as she moves swiftly and quietly to the other side of the room. She checks and adjusts the other patient's equipment, making notes on a chart clipped to the bed. When she finishes, instead of coming back to me, she returns to the workstation. I watch as she lowers herself out of sight.

I am woken by the sound of the double doors across the room swinging open. In walks my father with a man I don't know. My father is unshaven and looks worn out, but his face lights up when our eyes meet and he breaks into a trot. In moments he is by my side, flinging his arms around me before I can utter a single word…

I suddenly feel horribly dizzy. The room spins. My vision blurs. I am plunged into darkness. The dizziness stops but fear engulfs me. My vision returns. What I see makes no sense. I am sitting at a desk, looking at an unintelligible spreadsheet on a computer screen. The wall in front of me is one huge window. It is raining hard outside. The view reveals that I am in a high-rise building. Although it's daylight, the huge, steely grey clouds looming in the sky are dark and ominous.

Am I dreaming? Everything is so clear, so real. A phone starts to ring. It is next to a framed photograph I recognise. It is a picture of my mother and me, taken while we were on holiday in Thailand. Unbidden, my hand reaches out to pick up the phone but it is not my hand, not my arm. I try to wake myself up. Now is not the time to be drifting off but I can't bring myself out of this dream. I hold the receiver to my ear and say, "Hello?" This is not my voice, but I'd know it anywhere. I am dreaming that I am my father but somehow still aware that I am me. This is the strangest experience I have ever had. None of my dreams have ever felt like this.

"Mr. Page?" It is a man's voice. One I've never heard before.

"Yes, Aaron Page here."

"Detective Kalifeh here from Rose Bay Police Station. I'm terribly sorry to be calling under these circumstances but I need to inform you that there's been an accident..."

As suddenly as the dream began, it is over.

"Juno? Juno? Darling? Is she ok?"

My dad sounds terrified. His voice has grown in volume so much he is almost yelling. Someone is shining a light directly into my eyes.

"Dad, I'm fine," I say, trying to reassure him.

The doctor is standing between my father and me. He is about my father's age. Although he is smiling, I see the concern in his eyes.

"Juno, I'm Dr. Davis. I know you're anxious to speak with your father but I need to ask you a couple of questions first."

I nod, eager to get this over with.

"Do you have any idea why you are here?"

"I have no idea whatsoever, I don't know what's..."

I look to my father for help. Seeing the sadness etched in his face, the words die on my lips. The tears welling in his eyes start to spill over, running down his cheeks. Suddenly I am struck by a horrible memory. My mother, my beautiful mother is gone.

# Chapter 3

S he is gone. I can't stop crying. I feel like I have been kicked in the stomach repeatedly. One minute I can't believe she is no longer here, the next I am feeling hopeless at the thought of life without her. Out of nowhere, I am angrier than I have ever been. How can she have done this to me? How could she leave me like this? How can life be this unfair? As quickly as the anger came it is gone, leaving me desperate and scared. I feel like a tiny rudderless boat tossed around on a huge sea, anchored to nothing.

I wish I were back in the ICU. At least there were other patients, staff around the clock. Where is my father, why isn't he here? I am no longer hooked to anything. Mine is the only bed in the room. A window to my left looks out over the hospital grounds to the streets beyond. There is a brown armchair near my bed with a pillow, blanket and linen strewn on the seat. The walls are peach coloured, matching the curtains pulled back on either side of the bed. I still have so many questions; there are still so many things I don't understand.

There is a gentle knock on the door before it opens. A young nurse walks in. She is smiling openly at me. Like the other nurse, she looks gentle and kind. Perhaps that's just the way it is with all of them. She is very fair-skinned. Although she is wearing it pinned up under a regulation cap, her curly red hair escapes in wisps around her face. She speaks with a strong Irish accent.

"Hello Juno, I'm Rachel and I'm your nurse for today - well, until my shift ends anyway. Your Dad has just popped home for a shower. I virtually had to kick him out the door that worried he was about leaving your side. He should be back any time now. Dr. Davis was also here while you were sleeping and didn't want to disturb you, but he has given you the all clear to go home tomorrow. I'm just going to take your blood pressure, ok?"

I nod. She seems very nice, but with my world in tatters, I have no desire for small talk. She fits the apparatus onto my arm, taking hold of my wrist to record my pulse…

The room starts to spin. My vision clouds. I am in darkness. Within seconds, I can see clearly. I am in a sitting room I have never seen before. I am at the far end of a large, brown sofa, with a man I don't recognise who is sprawled on the rest of the available space. He has a full head of thick black hair, is broad-shouldered and looks like he spends time in the gym. Both arms are covered in sleeves of tattoos.

I am able to see the clothes I am wearing. Nothing looks even vaguely familiar. Thick red hair hangs down almost to my waist.

Through the only window in the room, I can tell it is daytime. There is a cricket match being shown on the largest plasma screen television I have ever seen.

"Blind Freddie could see that was wide. Bloody umpire!"

This is yelled at the television as though it might somehow be heard. The worrying thought that I may be going mad fills me with terror. What is happening to me? I am definitely not asleep. This cannot be a dream. Suddenly the person whose body I inhabit starts to speak.

"It's just that we are supposed to be meeting Michelle and Kevin for a drink."

The Irish accent is unmistakable. The man beside me lurches forward towards me and starts shouting.

"You stupid cow! All I ask for is a bit of peace so I can watch the match, and what I get instead is your non-stop bloody nagging!"

"But Zac, when we discussed it last night you were fine with it."

This is spoken softly, hesitantly. The words are no sooner spoken when without warning, a clenched fist comes towards me. A hot knot of pain twists through my right upper arm and shoulder. The person I have become recoils into a ball, one hand clutching the injured arm, the other protecting her face...

I hear my name repeated over and over. I open my eyes to find Nurse Rachel hovering over me, staring anxiously at me.

"Juno, are you alright?"

"Yes." I reply immediately but my voice does not sound convincing even to me.

"Oh, you gave me a start. I thought we'd gone and lost you again."

She is smiling with relief, though still clearly shaken. I am not sure if it's the right thing to do but part of me has to know, needs to understand what is going on. I raise my hand, placing it gently on her right upper arm, watching her face closely as I speak.

"Does it still hurt?"

Her reaction is all the answer I need. The smile on her face disappears, replaced by a look of bewilderment. This only lasts fleetingly. The thing I see in her eyes as she backs away from me and out of the room, is fear.

# Chapter 4

What is happening to me? Only last night, when Dad hugged me, I was in his office, receiving a call that would shatter his world. Today, a nurse takes my pulse, transporting me to her living room, where a horrible bully hit me. It didn't happen when I first saw Dad, or Nurse Rachel. Nothing at all happened with the nurse in the ICU, or with Dr. Davis. I can't make sense of it, of anything. My mind is spinning. Then it dawns on me. It only happened when they touched me.

There is a gentle knock on the door. It opens and Dad walks in, carrying a bag.

"Hi Dad."

I quickly pull the blankets up to my chin, hoping if he touches me through them, I might be safe.

"Hello angel, how are you feeling? Are you cold? Here, have an extra blanket."

Placing the bag down, he scoops up a blanket from the chair next to my bed and drapes it over me. He leans down to kiss my cheek. I close my eyes in anticipation, trying hard not to look as though I am about to be bitten by a cobra. I feel a little dizzy, but this could easily be anxiety. It recedes as soon as the kiss is over.

"You're allowed to come home tomorrow."

The tone of his voice is far cheerier than either of us feels. We look at each other, both understanding that 'home' no longer means what it once did. I imagine him wondering what is safe to say, and what should never be talked about again.

"I brought you some clothes, I hope they're ok." He gestures to the bag at the foot of the bed.

"We'll get through this Juno, together. It isn't going to be easy, but we still have each other. I know I'm not your mother, but I will do everything in my power to take care of you. I promise."

The tears start to come, but the thought of him hugging me, the fear that I will disappear into another world, is enough to stop them. I bite the inside of my mouth, something I do to keep myself from crying. I have the rest of my life for sadness. Right now there are some things I need to find out. I swallow a couple of times to be sure the tears are far enough away for me to speak.

"Dad, I know there was an accident, but I still don't know why I'm here. I don't seem to have a bruise on me, so I couldn't have been with Mum."

"No sweetheart, you weren't in the car. Dr. Davis explained this might happen. He said you might suffer from partial or even complete amnesia for events surrounding the accident."

Amnesia is something I've heard of. Mainly from those ridiculous daytime soaps my grandmother Rosie watches. I never imagined it might be something that would happen to me. Then again, I had never imagined that my mother would die.

"He said any memory you lost as a result of the shock would almost certainly return. So don't get stressed about it, ok?"

He looks so worried; in fact he looks absolutely terrible. I don't think the bags under his swollen, bloodshot eyes or his new beard are helping.

"Ok." I smile, trying to reassure myself as much as him.

"So why *am* I here?"

"I received a phone call from a detective to let me know there had been a car accident and that Lily was in the hospital."

This I already know all too well, but I remain silent.

"When I got to the hospital the doctor who operated on your mum sat with me and explained what had happened. I took in very little of what he said. None of it mattered anyway. By that time she was already gone. I phoned home but you weren't there. In hindsight, that was a blessing. It was a stupid idea. I really don't know what I was thinking, what I would have said had you answered. As if something like that can be told over the phone."

Unwanted thoughts of mobile phones come to me. If I owned a mobile phone, he would have been able to contact me no matter where I was. This had been the biggest bone of contention between my mother and I since I'd turned thirteen. Mum had very strong beliefs about certain things and mobile phones were one of them. Dad continues talking, bringing me out of my reverie.

"Telling you about the accident was the hardest thing I have ever done. You immediately fainted. At least that's what I thought had happened, but you didn't come around. No matter what I tried, I couldn't get you to wake up. We called an ambulance and that's how you ended up here. I have never been so terrified. The doctor called it a dissociative stupor. He said it was caused by the acute stress you experienced when I told you what had happened."

"How long was I out for?"

"Exactly two days, almost to the hour. The accident was on Friday, and you came round yesterday, which was Sunday. They were the two longest days I have ever lived through."

He stands, wanders over to the window, staring out at the streets below. When he starts speaking again it is very softly, almost as though he is talking to himself.

"I still don't understand why Lily was even in the car. I can't imagine why she would have shut Juno's so early on a Friday afternoon. It was one of the busiest times in the shop, even in wet weather."

Juno's is my mum's shop. It was like another child to her. Entering Juno's is like walking into a wonderful dream, filled with soft colours, flowing fabrics and flowery scents. Juno's sells only beautiful things, no matter what they are, covering everything from jewellery, candles, silk bedspreads, quirky furniture and most things in between.

"Where was I?"

"You'd been shopping with Georgie. You both walked in looking so happy. I was sitting in the lounge, knowing that what I was about to tell you was going to break your heart."

Memory comes flooding back. Georgie asked me to go shopping with her to buy shoes for the party that weekend. I'd called Mum during lunch from Georgie's phone to let her know my plans. To ask her to collect my dress from the dry cleaners, in case I couldn't make it before closing. It had all seemed so important at the time.

Suddenly, the wind is out of me. It feels like someone has dropped a cement block on my chest. That's why Mum closed Juno's early on Friday. She did it for me. It is my fault that she was in the car so early on Friday afternoon. It is my fault that she is gone.

The tears come now. I am powerless to stop them. Dad rushes over, sitting on my bed, looking anxiously at me. He doesn't know what to do, and while a hug would be great, I am not sure I deserve one. Regardless, I am terrified at the thought, in case touching him sends me spinning off to somewhere even more horrible. I stay huddled under my blanket, making no attempt to reach for him. I understand that he thinks I am crying because of Mum, and while I am, it is guilt that is overwhelming me right now. This is not something I can confess, now or ever. How could he forgive me?

# Chapter 5

Exhausted after a sleepless night, I can't stop thinking about the day before Mum's accident. We were all at breakfast, as usual, when Mum announced that she had made dinner reservations for the three of us, at the local Italian place, Gary's. The restaurant is actually called 'La Piazza', but the owner is a lovely man named Gary and for that reason, the only name we have ever called it is 'Gary's'. We normally only ever went there for birthdays or other important celebrations.

"What's the special occasion?" I remember Dad asking.

"Why should we need a special occasion to enjoy each other's company and have a nice evening out together?" Mum asked, smiling broadly.

"Fair enough," said Dad – there really was no point arguing with Mum once her mind was set on something.

"Sounds lovely, I'll meet you two there after work."

At the time, thoughts of homework arose, but something made me stay quiet. It occurred to me then that maybe Mum just needed a night off from cooking.

The weather was perfect, so Mum had suggested we leave early and walk to the restaurant rather than drive. She had linked her arm through mine and we talked the whole way there. It's not as if we didn't talk every day but there was something different about this uninterrupted stretch of time. Just the two of us, no phones, no Dad, nobody and nothing but us. We talked about things that we didn't touch on often: her childhood, Rosie's illness, my future. At the time it didn't seem strange, just wonderful. Now, in hindsight, it is almost as though Mum had an inkling that time was running out.

Dad was at the table when we arrived and Gary was working that night, which always made for a better experience. The food was delicious as always. I realise now that Mum talked less than was normal for her. Instead of amusing us in her typical way, she asked interesting and searching questions of us both, drawing us out more.

After dinner, instead of eating dessert there as we normally did, Mum suggested we walk to an ice creamery that had recently opened to rave reviews. We each ordered huge double-scooped cones, piled high with gourmet concoctions, and ate them as we meandered home. The sky was an inky black dotted with hundreds of stars. We stopped in our front drive, star-gazing to search for the Southern Cross, something we had done since I was very small.

Thinking back now, if I had to create the perfect last night for the three of us, I couldn't have done much better. Right now, rather than

18

being grateful for this beautiful memory, I am overcome with remorse. My culpability is something I can't escape.

I go to the bathroom to change, taking the bag of clothes Dad has brought me. From the moment I understood that Mum's accident was my fault I have had the oddest feeling in my stomach. It is as though I have eaten something incredibly heavy, like a large stone. Instead of it being digested, it is sitting whole and untouched in the pit of my belly. With the knowledge that Mum's death is my fault also comes the belief that I have no right to wallow in grief. I know that it is my job to be strong for my father. He is the innocent victim here.

Sitting on the bed waiting for Dad in the outfit he brought for me, it is hard not to smile. If these were the last clothes in my wardrobe, Mum would still not have chosen them. The top is a T-shirt I made in Kid's Club on a holiday in Fiji, almost six years ago. It is yellow, blue and green tie-dye. It swam on me at the time. Now it is far too small. I am sure the only reason it was never tossed out is because I made it. Mum never liked to throw away anything I made, accounting for the endless boxes of my artwork, dating back to pre-school scribbles, still stored in the attic. The skirt is pink cotton, covered in multi-coloured polka dots. My grandmother Rosie gave it to me, which is why I still have it.

Rosie is in a nursing home now - the incongruously named Greenfields. She gave me this skirt for my fourteenth birthday over two years ago. The only other time I have worn it was the day she gave it to me. I never expected to wear it again. It's only due to the elasticised waist that I can wear it at all. I hope Dad parks close to the hospital so as few people as possible catch sight of me in it. Thinking about Rosie makes me realise I have been so wrapped up in my own situation; I haven't even considered how she is coping with the loss of my mother, her only child. Or if she is even aware Lily is gone.

Rosie is the most wonderful person I know. She moved in with us when I was just a baby. My grandfather had passed away six years before, and Rosie was spending so much time visiting us or babysitting me that moving in with us was a natural progression.

About five years ago she started having nightmares, causing her to shout and scream at night. When Mum, Dad or I reached her room, she had either stopped and was sleeping peacefully, or still yelling but actually asleep, unable to be consoled no matter what we did.

Sometimes, in an attempt to help, we upset her more. So we learnt to wait, watching until it passed. Eventually we didn't even go to her, just lay in our own beds waiting for her to stop. Although it was initially worrying, she always seemed totally fine in the morning. When we broached the subject, she had no recollection of any bad dreams at all. It continued for so long, happening at least once a week, that we all grew accustomed to it. Soon we stopped worrying altogether.

After a couple of years there were some other changes. Nothing much to begin with, just plain old forgetfulness that we are all guilty of at times. Things got a bit worse. She would be absolutely fine for days, and then she would be muddled and confused, sometimes for very short periods, occasionally for a couple of days. It began to be worrying. After much discussion an appointment was made to see our General Practitioner Dr. Richmond. He has been our family doctor for years, treating Rosie when she was a young mother. He is the reason that I have wanted to be a doctor for as long as I can remember. When Rosie moved into Greenfields, and I no longer needed to spend Saturdays keeping an eye on Rosie, I began working in his surgery.

Having examined Rosie, he was concerned enough to refer her to a neurologist. Following a seemingly endless battery of tests, we were told that she probably had a syndrome named Lewy Body Dementia. It was the onset of hallucinations about two years ago that finally cemented the specialist's opinion, confirming his diagnosis. The hallucinations, while sometimes absolutely harmless, were occasionally terrifying for Rosie.

With Mum at Juno's, Dad at work and me in school, it became increasingly difficult for us to look after Rosie. Eventually we hired a lady named Astrid to take care of her during the day. She was a retired nurse, a lovely woman. Astrid was older than Mum. She had never been married and had no children. Her sunny disposition made her a wonderful companion for Rosie. Their relationship was more like one between friends than one between carer and patient. I was often the first one home to relieve Astrid. Although her workday ended when I arrived, she often lingered, reading to Rosie or, on one of her good days, playing gin rummy or chatting over a cup of tea.

Sadly after caring for Rosie for just over a year, Astrid had to go interstate to a sister that needed her. We managed for a while with Mum getting help in the shop and me discontinuing some after school activities. We all knew it wouldn't work forever. It took Rosie falling down the stairs, breaking her hip one terrifying day last June, to force our hand. After looking around at all the available options, Greenfields stood out as the best solution for Rosie's needs.

Every Sunday for the past ten months we have driven to Greenfields to visit Rosie. Sometimes we go home wondering why we even bothered, as she seems to have no idea who we are, often confusing us for relatives and friends long since passed away. At other times, it is as though there has never been anything wrong with her, leaving us feeling guilty for not taking her home with us.

I recognise Dad's footsteps in the hall. I am standing before he enters the room. He has shaven and though he looks better this way, he looks sadder, more vulnerable somehow, even childlike. I am struck by an instinct to protect him so strong, I have to fight not to jump up and put my arms around him, like a mother would an injured child.

"I hope those clothes are ok?"

Even Dad has realised how ridiculous I look. When my smile becomes a chuckle, he starts to laugh too. Soon we are both laughing hard. It feels so good I almost start to cry. Still laughing, Dad explains how he came to choose my clothes.

"They were together in your cupboard when everything else was separated into tops and bottoms. I couldn't trust myself to pick things that would go well together. So I took the easy option, picking the ready made outfit."

Eventually our laughter subsides and we face each other still smiling.

"Everything will be ok Dad. We'll be ok."

I am not sure who I am trying to convince but I feel better having spoken the words. They seem to positively affect Dad too.

He opens the door for me. As we walk into the corridor, he places his hand on the small of my back. This is surely meant as a calming gesture, but has the opposite effect on me. My pace immediately quickens, just enough to keep his hand from touching me. I cannot imagine how I am going to keep this up, but for the moment it seems the only thing to do. We stop at the nurses' station for Dad to sign paperwork. Glancing around, I hope to spot Nurse Rachel, who I have not laid eyes on since yesterday. She is nowhere to be seen.

Arriving into the empty elevator, I am careful to stand at the back to avoid touching anyone else who might enter. Two floors down the doors open. A young couple steps in. He is holding a car capsule in one hand and his partner's hand in the other. The capsule contains a newborn baby dressed in a pink all-in-one with matching bonnet and booties. Her tiny hands are curled into fists. Her full pink lips are pursed. She is sleeping peacefully. The couple stands close together, barely taking their eyes off their new daughter. They look so incredibly happy. It makes my heart hurt. It is hard not to be pleased for them, but impossible to miss the glaring contrast between our circumstances. They are going home with a new life. We are going home to a lost one.

We are both quiet during the drive home. It would normally be unheard of for us to drive any distance at all without the radio, or our iPod blaring. Neither of us makes a move to turn the music on. Mum adored music and knew the words to thousands of songs, belting them out loudly as we drove. Dad and I used to join in, mostly during the choruses, happily listening to Mum sing the various verses. Singing was one of her favourite past-times, second only to dancing.

Nothing cheered me up more than walking in the door to find Mum dancing around the kitchen to Oasis, Pink or Jason Mraz. When I was younger, there was nothing more embarrassing than having my friends watch as Mum spun around the kitchen, singing as she went. As I grew up, I noticed how my friends loved Mum, enjoying her antics. Sophie, Georgie and Izzy all have nice mothers, but none seemed as fun or as vital as mine. Mum's initials were L.P, Georgie once joked that this actually stood for Life of the Party.

As we turn into our street, what strikes me most is that everything looks the same. It seems impossible that my life could have changed so dramatically yet there be no evidence in the physical world. We turn into our driveway. Though the engine is off, I make no move to open my door. Dad is up and out, removing a bag of groceries from the boot, opening my door for me. I follow him up the path to our front door and into the house.

Again, I am startled by the fact that while everything has changed, nothing has. The furniture all looks the same, as do the pictures on the walls. Dad walks straight through the living room to the kitchen, busily unpacking and putting away groceries. I notice all the vases of flowers dotted here and there. They are mostly white, a few pale pinks and yellows mixed in. Clearly people feel bright colours are to be avoided in a house of mourning. This is kind of crazy when you think about it. Surely sad people need bright, colourful things to cheer them up? Walking into the dining room I see more flowers. The house resembles a funeral parlour.

My room is the same as always but neater. It is clear that Mrs. De Jong, or Mrs. Young as I have called her since I was very small, has been while I was in hospital. Mrs. Young is a gorgeous Dutch lady who worked as a full-time housekeeper for my grandmother when she was a young mother, running her own boutique clothing store. When my grandmother retired about fifteen years ago, moving in with us, Mrs. Young retired too, working with us one Saturday a fortnight. I am sure it was a desire to stay close to our family, rather than financial need, that kept her working.

I am sitting on the bed when Dad walks in. He stands in front of me with his arms open. I have absolutely no choice but to go to him. Part of me is terrified, part of me is curious; the rest of me is resigned. With his arms around me, I am only momentarily dizzy. An enormous wave of relief washes over me. I hug him harder to be absolutely sure. Still nothing happens. It is wonderful to be able to touch him without careening off into some other world. Does this mean I am better, that I can touch anyone and have nothing happen?

We pull apart but remain holding hands. As Dad begins to speak, he sits on my bed gesturing for me to do the same. There are tears in his eyes. He works hard to keep them there.

"Juno, the funeral is set for tomorrow afternoon."

Funeral? It hadn't occurred to me. Of course there has to be a funeral. That's what happens when someone dies.

"Right. Of course."

What else is there to say? I feel like screaming. I don't feel ready for a funeral. I don't feel ready to say goodbye.

I have never even been to a funeral. My third class teacher lost a husband to cancer when I was eight. My parents went to the service without me, explaining that funerals weren't for children. At twelve, they still deemed me too young to go to Sophie's grandmother's funeral. Sadly I am no longer a child. Even if I was, I guess this is one funeral that I can't miss. I wish with all my heart that I could. The boulder in the pit of my stomach helps to remind me it is my fault that Lily is gone. The least I can do is be strong enough to attend her funeral, to help Dad get through the day.

"I have arranged for a non-religious service. It will be carried out at the crematorium. It's what she would have wanted. I am going to go to Greenfields to collect Rosie tomorrow morning so that she can come with us. I'd love you to come with me, but you don't have to."

"Have you seen her?"

"I was there on Sunday. I was on my way back from there when Dr. Davis called to tell me you were awake."

"How was she?"

"It wasn't one of her better days."

"But did she understand? I mean, does she know?"

"I have no idea. I wasn't here on the Friday night when she called because I was at the hospital with you. I called and spoke with her on Saturday. I hated giving her the news over the phone but I was worried she would have a run of bad days, possibly lasting beyond the funeral. When I got to Greenfields on Sunday she was having a bad day. The staff said they would definitely explain things to her if she had a good day, and seemed unaware of what had happened."

He smiles sadly before standing and making for the door.

# Chapter 6

I must have fallen asleep, waking with a start at the sound of the telephone's shrill ring. It only rings twice before stopping. My heart is still beating a little too fast when moments later, Dad knocks lightly before opening my bedroom door, holding the phone in front of him.

"It's for you, it's Georgie."

I love Georgie enormously, but right now I don't feel like talking to anybody. My face clearly gives this away, and sensing my reticence he adds in a whisper,

"She's been very worried about you."

My body feels heavy, slow, sapped of energy, which is crazy when I have done nothing but lie in bed for the past four days. Trying hard not to think about the conversation ahead of me I take the phone.

"Hi George."

"Oh Juno, you poor thing, I'm so sorry, what an appalling thing to happen to you, to Lily, she was so gorgeous, we all loved her so much. Your Dad looked so sad, the whole thing was just so horrible. I couldn't believe what I was hearing. I was absolutely terrified when you fainted like that. You wouldn't wake up. It was awful. Then the ambulance came, you looked so dreadful lying on the stretcher like that. I wanted to come and see you in hospital, well we all did, but they wouldn't let us. We were so worried about you. Do you want me to come over now? It's easy if you do. It's ok if you don't, I understand, just tell me what you want me to do."

All this is said with no hint of a pause. This is classic Georgie. Where most would be tongue-tied, worried about finding the right words, Georgie has no such qualms, instead finding it hard to stop talking. She is the youngest of five children, which explains why she always talks so fast. She has spent her whole life squeezing her words into the gaps between those of her parents and siblings. Talking this way has become a habit. Spending time at Georgie's house is always an incredibly loud, hugely entertaining event.

"I do feel awful, George. I hope you'll never ever feel this way but it is so good to hear your voice."

"Do you want me to come over? I can get off the bus right now and be at yours in five?"

"Thanks George, but no. I think Dad and I need to be alone, at least for now."

Dad finds Georgie's ceaseless chatter trying at the best of times. I can't imagine how he would cope with her boundless energy right now.

"Ok. I'll be there tomorrow though, I promise. Mr. Fitzgerald called a special assembly today and announced that any students who feel they want to show you their support by attending the funeral can take the afternoon off. He has even arranged a bus to drive students there."

The thought of all those people tomorrow is horrifying. A wave of nausea washes over me.

"Sorry, George I've got to go."

"Ok, see you tomorrow, love you."

Lying back on my bed, waiting for the nausea to pass, I remember that I didn't touch the awful hospital breakfast offered to me hours ago. Once I am feeling slightly better, I make my way to the kitchen for something to eat. Passing Dad in the lounge, I offer to make him a late lunch. I notice a couple of Tupperware containers and a casserole dish in the fridge that aren't ours. People have clearly done more than just send flowers.

I put together a platter of olives, cheese, avocado and crackers. Instead of sitting in our usual seats at the table, which now looks bigger than ever, we sit at the kitchen counter. Although the food looks fine, neither of us eats with any gusto. We are nearly finished clearing away when the phone rings again. Since I learned to talk, my position as our family's designated phone answerer has gone unquestioned. Things have changed; my desire to rush to the phone has entirely vanished. Dad picks up the kitchen extension.

"Hello."

As he hears the caller's voice, he turns to look at me. I correctly assume the call is for me. I can only hear Dad's end of the conversation, but it isn't hard to decipher the rest.

"Hi Sophie, yes, she's home."

"She seems to be doing ok."

"Yes, you're right it will take time."

"Yes, she was a wonderful person."

On the word 'was' his voice catches but he manages, after a pause, to finish the sentence. In a voice that is almost a whisper, he continues.

"Lily loved you too."

"Yes, we got it. Please thank Annie for me."

"Yes, we'll see you all tomorrow."

"She's right here, I'll put her on."

Taking the phone, I can't help but notice the tears in his eyes. Sophie is my oldest friend. Our parents have known each other since before we were born. We grew up on opposite sides of the same street. Sophie's family moved to a bigger house four years ago when they discovered Annie, Sophie's mum, was pregnant with twins, but even now we live within walking distance of each other.

Dad gestures for me to stop clearing up and leave it for him. I thank him, making my way to my room.

"Hi Soph."

"Juno, how are you?"

That's all it takes, four words, spoken by my oldest friend. In that instant all my defences come down. Thankfully, I have reached my room, and am able to close the door behind me, before the first huge sobs tear through me. Unable to speak, I cradle the phone to my ear, curling myself into a ball on my bed. Sophie says nothing, but sensing her there on the other end keeps me from totally giving in to my grief. After what seems like a very long time my sobbing abates.

> "Juno, losing Lily like that is just about the most horrible thing that I can ever imagine happening to you. This may not be the best time to say this, but I love you like a sister and want you to know that even though she is not here with you in a physical form, she is still with you and always will be."

Sophie is the spiritual one among us. I have never given much thought to souls and what happens to people after they die but it has been a topic that Sophie has had definite opinions about ever since her grandmother passed away four years ago. Sophie was extremely close to her grandmother who died after suffering a major stroke, just months before Sophie's twin siblings were born.

Sophie was distraught for weeks. One morning, upon opening her front door, she discovered a book on the doormat. It was titled *Journey of Souls* and after reading it, Sophie was certain that her grandmother's soul was very much alive. Moreover, she believed her grandmother was somehow responsible for getting the book to her. It didn't help that whoever had left the book, wrote nothing in it, attached no note, nor ever mentioned it to either Sophie or Annie.

> "I'm not telling you not to cry, because that would be wrong, you need to cry bucket loads. What I am telling you is that she isn't gone from you in every sense of the word."

Normally, when Sophie goes off on a 'spiritual rant', as Georgie calls them, I switch off; today I listen.

> "As I am talking to you now, I can feel her. I feel her so strongly it is as though she is standing here with me, but I know I am only feeling her because of how strongly she is with *you* right now."

Closing my eyes, I try to feel what Sophie is feeling, I try to feel my mother around me, to get a sense of her near me. I fail miserably.

> "Thanks, Soph."

> "You believe me, don't you?"

> "Yes, of course I do."

I am not lying. Sophie means everything she is saying. Therefore it is true. True for her anyway.

> "I'm sorry, Soph, I'm absolutely shattered. I'll see you tomorrow, ok?"

> "Yes of course, I'm sorry Juno, I shouldn't be prattling on about all this, at least not now. If you feel like talking at all, I mean ever, just pick up the phone. Get some rest. I'll see you tomorrow."

> "Thanks again, Soph, bye."

When the phone rings half an hour later, I don't need to answer it to know it's Izzy. I ask Dad to let it go to the answering machine. I don't feel up to speaking with anyone else today. I know she and her family will be there tomorrow.

The rest of the day passes quietly. We eat lasagna, kindly made by a neighbour, with no more relish than we did lunch. The stone in my stomach seems to leave little room for food.

Despite having done nothing more strenuous than make lunch, I collapse into bed exhausted. Normally I am one of those lucky people who fall asleep as their head hits the pillow. Tonight, despite feeling shattered, sleep eludes me.

I can't stop thinking about the call I made to Mum. Why had I been so selfish? Why hadn't I just told Georgie that we had to be done by five o'clock, so I could collect the dress? I ask myself these questions over and over until finally sleep claims me.

# Chapter 7

We set off for Greenfields around 10am hoping to be back in time for lunch. Sitting in the front seat next to Dad feels so wrong. This is Mum's seat. Our visits to Rosie are a ritual and this just isn't my position. The drive usually takes about forty-five minutes. The weather is perfect with the morning chill gone and a clear blue sky above.

I try to think of something to say, to punctuate the silence. Dad turns the radio on and I no longer have to worry. When *Hot 'N' Cold* by Katy Perry comes on, he turns to smile at me. He taps out the beat on the steering wheel, humming along with the melody. Mum would have been singing along loudly. I am content to close my eyes, imagining I can hear her voice, just as it would sound if she were here. Dad is working so hard to act normal. It is important I play along.

Having parked the car, we walk up the stairs to the entrance. All the staff know us, and the woman at reception, phone pressed to her ear, smiles as we walk towards her. Her face is laced with sympathy, a clear sign she has heard about Mum. I have never considered before how many different types of smiles there are. How long will it be before I can no longer detect sympathy or sadness in the smiles I receive? She indicates she may be some time. Dad tells me to go ahead while he sorts out the paperwork required to take Rosie out for the day.

I find Rosie sitting in the sun on the balcony, off the lounge. As soon as our eyes meet, I know immediately how she is. Either I see the Rosie I know and love staring at me, into me. Or I see that other Rosie, the uncertain, hesitant one, looking furtive, almost afraid of whom I might be. Today I see my Rosie, the one who knows and loves me. One look is enough to know she is aware of what has happened, and why I am here. I walk towards her, my eyes brimming with tears. I kneel down in front of her. As I begin to cry, I bury my head in her lap, wrapping my arms around her waist...

Without warning, it happens again. The darkness and dizziness last only briefly. I find myself sitting in the lounge I have only moments ago walked through. I know without looking that the body I am in belongs to Rosie. There are about a dozen other people in the room. A couple of them are on a couch facing the television, watching a cooking program. Some are reading newspapers. A lady I have seen many times before looks, as always, like she is playing an imaginary harp. Several others are dozing in chairs.

Rosie is playing cards with a man sitting opposite. It is her friend Eric. He and his son and daughter-in-law, Bruce and Claire have joined us for Sunday lunch several times at Greenfields. Rosie is about to play her turn when the cards held in Eric's left hand unexpectedly drop to the table. He seems as though he may be about to speak, but his face becomes a grimace of pain. Rosie yells for help. A male nurse rushes over, arriving just as Eric's head slumps forward, protected from hitting the table by his own arms...

My head is still lying in Rosie's lap. She is stroking my hair, singing a song. The same one she has sung to me whenever I felt sad, as far back as I can remember.

"I'd do anything, for you, dear, anything, for you. You know why? Because I love you."

I raise my head. Our eyes meet. She stops singing. Rosie has always been able to read me like a book.

"Oh, Juno, my darling, you poor girl. I know you must be feeling absolutely dreadful right now. I wish I could take the pain away. Sadly I can't, but I can promise that eventually things will get easier. I know that's difficult to believe right now, but in time things will get better."

Understandably, Rosie has misattributed the fear in my face.

"Rosie?"

"Yes, Juno."

"Is Eric alright?"

Rosie's surprise is evident. She slowly nods her head, eyes boring into mine.

"Yes, he's going to be fine. The doctors say he had a heart attack, but he's as strong as an ox. He'll be back on his feet in no time. He is in hospital, apparently doing very well, considering it only happened a few days ago."

Her voice starts to falter a little. The last few words are spoken in a hushed tone. She looks intently at me, looking right through me.

"Did somebody tell you?"

Her tone implies she already knows the answer. I shake my head very slowly, afraid to talk.

"So how did you know?"

This is whispered. If there is one person in the world I can talk to about this madness, it is Rosie. I feel a desperate need to talk to someone. However, I have no idea what to say, how to explain what is happening. Part of me is relieved when we are interrupted by Dad's arrival.

"Morning, Mum, how are you feeling today?"

His eyes move between Rosie's and mine. His question aimed at both of us. Like me, Dad had feared today might be one of Rosie's bad days. The plan to take her to Mum's funeral might have needed to be abandoned. I give him a look, which he knows means all is well. Rosie is herself. Rosie's eyes linger on mine a little longer, before turning her gaze to Dad.

"I'm fine, Aaron, all things considered. How are you doing?"

"I'm very relieved to have Juno home."

They both look at me. Their love for me is palpable. Would they still feel this way if they knew Mum's accident was my fault?

"Do you need help getting your things together?" Dad asks Rosie.

"No thank you, I'm all organised, ready to leave when you are."

"Let's make a move then."

The forced lightness of his tone makes it sound like we are off to a country picnic, rather than to bury our beloved Lily.

Together, we help Rosie out of her chair. As we touch, I feel faintly dizzy. This fades rapidly. A look passes between us. It is understood that our conversation will be continued. On our way to Rosie's room to collect her bag, she reaches for my arm to steady her. This time, as we touch, I feel nothing. It is strange, and difficult to understand. Why does touching someone send me spinning back in time, yet, at other times, touching that same person has no effect on me?

When we arrive at the car, I open the front door for Rosie. Once she is safely seated, I climb into the back seat. Dad turns the music down so we can talk. Rosie tells the story about Eric's heart attack, as though our conversation never happened. Dad asks enough questions for both of us, so I need not act too surprised. Rosie continues with a steady stream of chatter until we are home.

I spend the time trying to devise a survival guide for the day. The thought of having to farewell my mother is devastating enough. Add the terrifying thought of scores of witnesses. How many of them will I have to touch? How many times will I be sucked into someone else's body to witness some horrible scene?

It is almost midday when we pull into our driveway. At this exact moment a new thought occurs to me. Every time I have flipped into someone else's memory, I have either been lying or sitting down. What will happen if I am standing up at the time? Will I collapse? Weirder still, will I be left standing like a statue? These thoughts are so horrifying that for a while, I am unable to move. Thankfully, the time it takes for Dad to help Rosie out is enough for me to calm down. I console myself with the thought that if ever there is a day when people will understand me being a little weird, it is today. What happens after today, I will worry about later.

Lunch is much the same as yesterday. Rosie being with us means we sit at the table, both making more of an effort at conversation. Rosie is amazing, despite the fact she must be suffering as much as us. Somehow she manages to be chatty, engaging us both without necessitating much response. The undigested lump in the pit of my stomach has markedly reduced my appetite. Neither Dad nor Rosie seems to notice.

Clearing away after lunch, I hear a car engine and I am stunned when a large black limousine pulls into our driveway. Parked behind our tiny car, it looks huge, alien and imposing. It is utterly out of place in our garden on this perfectly beautiful day. I hadn't thought about how we would get to the funeral. I guess this is what happens. It makes sense that Dad does not want to drive to the funeral. I watch as a uniformed gentleman climbs out of the car, and gazing at his reflection, adjusts his hat.

The sight of the hearse has turned my legs to jelly. With enormous effort, I move away from the sink towards the lounge, to let Dad know the car is here. The doorbell rings, saving me from speech. Dad has already answered the door by the time I am in the living room. It is he that tells me the time has come.

The driver introduces himself as Richard, offering us his condolences. Before long we are all sitting in the elegantly appointed car. Rosie and I face forward, Dad opposite us, his back to Richard. Whenever our eyes meet, Dad smiles. I genuinely attempt to smile back but my stomach is churning thinking of all the people I may have to touch today. To distract myself, I turn to stare out the window at people enjoying an ordinary Wednesday. Right now, it is hard to imagine I will ever have one again. I remind myself that if it weren't for me, none of this would have happened. I renew my resolve to be strong for Dad, promising myself not to fall apart today.

# Chapter 8

Arriving at the crematorium we are greeted by three staff. They are all incredibly solicitous without being overbearing. Dad is gently led away by two of them. The third, named Neil, shows Rosie and me to the main room. The sight of the coffin is another thing I am not mentally prepared for. I am momentarily stunned. Rosie senses my horror. With her arm around me, we walk to the front row. A wave of nausea grips me as we sit. I will myself to be strong. The nausea ebbs, leaving me terribly cold. I am hugely relieved when Dad sits next to me, putting his arm around me, sandwiching me between them.

Sitting safely between Rosie and Dad, I risk a glance at the coffin. It is dark red wood, polished to a shine, with matte silver rather than glossy handles, not at all ornate. I know Mum would have chosen something similar herself had she been able to. This comforts me. I can now look at the coffin. However, the minute I imagine Lily lying there and think about what the accident might have done to her, the nausea instantly returns, worse than before. I begin to shiver and shake. I catch Dad and Rosie looking at each other. They both rub my back until my teeth stop chattering, my body stops quivering. I cannot remember ever wanting a day to be over more than this one.

The sound of the door opening at the rear of the room causes Dad to stir. Rosie remains unmoved. In keeping with my resolve to be strong, on shaky legs, I begin to stand.

"Aaron, darling, would you mind terribly if Juno stayed here with me?" Rosie asks taking hold of my hand.

"Of course not," he replies, leaning forward, planting a kiss on the top of my head, before walking down the aisle.

Is it possible Rosie intentionally saved me? Regardless, relief courses through me. I squeeze her hand in thanks, resting my head on her shoulder.

I hear hushed voices as people convey their condolences. Mourners are arriving at a steady pace. Having spoken with Dad, most are content to take a seat somewhere, however Annie and Sophie make their way to the front. My eyes remain trained on my lap.

Annie is like a second mother, Sophie like a sister. Just the sight of them would cause me to dissolve. I can't let it happen. Annie kneels in front of Rosie and letting go of my hand, Rosie clasps Annie's hands in both of hers. Sophie stands in front of me. My heart pounds, the nausea has returned. I feel totally unprepared for today. Short of wearing a suit of armour, I don't know what I could have done to prepare better.

Closing my eyes, I determinedly slow down my breathing, trying to regain some sense of composure. Keeping my eyes closed, my head bowed, I work to get myself under control. When I open my eyes, Sophie and Annie are still there. Sophie now has her arm extended in front of her mother, keeping her from getting any closer to me. Sophie is the most sensitive person I know. She has clearly intuited my need for space. Risking a glance up at them, I read the hurt in Annie's expression. I smile wanly, trying to show my appreciation. She smiles back, her confusion evident. She turns allowing Sophie to gently guide her away. Sophie looks over her shoulder as they leave, her smile one of complete empathy.

Organ music is playing. People are deliberately trying to be quiet, but the level of noise in the room is substantial. Despite this, I distinctly hear Georgie's arrival. I cannot hear Sophie but I know she has stopped George rushing up to me.

"Are you sure, Sophie? She may want us there with her."

The rest of the exchange is lost. Again I am grateful for Sophie's thoughtfulness. Dad returns, sitting by my side, taking my hand in his. Rosie takes my other hand in hers as Neil, the man who greeted us earlier, takes the stage.

He introduces himself, welcomes everybody, and begins to talk generally about losing a loved one. I can't help wondering if it is something he has experienced himself. Eventually he begins to talk about my mother. It seems absurd listening to the details, however accurate, of my mother's life, told by a man I am certain she never met. He covers her childhood, school and university careers, and marriage to Dad. He mentions my birth and the opening of Juno's five years later. Then he announces that Lily's husband Aaron will deliver the eulogy.

Dad smiles sadly down at me, disengaging his hand from my grip. I am bewildered until I realise with a start what is happening. Dad is going to stand up there and talk in front of all these people. I feel foolish for not knowing this would happen. He has to talk. Who else is there to do it? My wonderful father walks up the stairs, faces the room, preparing to talk.

Up there alone, he looks small, defenceless. It is difficult to watch. His head is bowed, making it hard to read his expression. I know him well. He is steadying himself to speak without crying. Everyone waits patiently. He raises his head, looking directly at me before beginning.

"Thank you all so much for coming. Many of you already know this story so I'll keep it brief. I first laid eyes upon Lily Dixon in 1985 when we were both aged sixteen. We met on her mother Rosie's front porch. I had a part-time job delivering firewood, and Lily was the one who answered the door that wonderful April afternoon. After I had completed the next two deliveries to the Dixon household, without so much as a glimpse of Lily, I staked out the house until I could pluck up the courage to speak to her. I knew from the first moment that this glorious, vibrant, intelligent woman was the one for me."

His voice quavers on this last sentence and he takes a few moments to recover before continuing.

"We eventually married in 1993 and Lily gave birth to our beautiful Juno the following year. Anyone who knew Lily understood how incredibly special she was. Lily could single-handedly light up a room. No matter how low you were feeling, just being in her presence instantly made your problems, no matter how large, seem manageable. I feel incredibly blessed to have shared twenty-five wonderful years with this amazing woman; my Lily, my best friend, my soulmate, my wife. Lily was a wonderful mother, devoted daughter and a cherished friend to many. She will be terribly missed.

"I found a poem that I believe expresses what Lily would say to us now if she could. I want to share it with you all.

*"When I leave you don't weep for me..."*

Here his voice catches. He begins to cry softly. It is heartbreaking watching him. Seizing this perfect opportunity to be strong for Dad, I turn to Rosie, letting go of her arm, stand, and walk to join him on the stage. Dad can't conceal his surprise or his relief at having me by his side. He puts his arm around me, handing me the poem. I look out at the sea of faces in front of me. Seeing so many people takes my breath away. I don't know why it surprises me; she was such a wonderful person. Looking at the piece of paper I hold, I take a few moments to compose myself. When I am ready, I read the poem my father selected to farewell my mother.

*When I leave you please do not cry*
*Share the wine & recall*
*How my laughter sounded*
*Look at each other and smile.*

*When it is your time to join me*
*Know that I will be there*
*I will wait for you*
*Take your time.*

Walking off the stage together we take our seats next to Rosie. Despite the tears streaming down her face, she manages to look both pleased and proud. She squeezes my hand to convey her approval.

Josh Groban's *To Where You Are* starts playing. Mum has always loved this song. This is no coincidence. Another thing Dad has arranged. I squeeze his arm hoping to show what a great job he has done. I have not been any help. Instead I have been another item on a long list of things for him to worry about.

Moments later, I notice the coffin gradually sliding backwards. Crimson velvet drapes I hadn't noticed before are moving inexorably towards each other from either side of the stage. Again I am struck by how stupid I have been, not having foreseen this moment. Perhaps the stupor I was in has had some lasting effect on me. Maybe some cognitive functioning has gone awry along with bits of my memory. The curtains move slowly but not slowly enough. The coffin disappears from view. This is the last time I will ever say goodbye to Mum.

When the music stops Dad stands. He looks down at me, trying to gauge whether I am capable of joining him to receive people's condolences. The look on my face, the way I grip Rosie's arm must be enough of an answer. He smiles sympathetically at me, turning to walk alone through the crowd. The room slowly empties. Rosie and I remain sitting together, clinging to one another, my head on her shoulder. Finally, Dad comes to tell us that we are alone. The three of us walk out together to the waiting car.

# Chapter 9

Everything seems hollow and grey. All that was bright, colourful and vibrant in the world has vanished, leaving behind a washed out vacuum.

The guilt is unbearable. At its best it's a boulder in my stomach. At worst it's a steel knife in my rib cage, making it hard to breathe. 'Where does it hurt?' Mum would have asked. It hurts everywhere, and it doesn't hurt enough.

Sleep is my only escape. The awful truth of what has happened seems yet to have pierced my subconscious. In my dreams Lily is there, as present and alive as ever. In those first few moments after waking it is as though nothing has happened. All is as it should be. Then reality comes crashing in. Nothing will ever be the same again.

Why am I alive while my beautiful mother is gone? If only I hadn't been so thoughtless, so wrapped up in myself, she would still be here with us. Dad would still have a wife. Rosie would still have a daughter. I would still have my mother.

I am crying again. Anger returns, flooding into me. What right do I have to be so self-pitying? This is my fault! I need to pull myself together, to be brave for Dad. I wash my face before going to look for him, finding him in the lounge room, curled up in the foetal position, occupying Mum's favourite spot on the sofa. He looks so innocent, so peaceful. It is hard to believe he is the same man I saw farewell his cherished wife only days ago.

The days pass in a blur. If not for the calendar hanging in the kitchen, I would have no idea what day it is. The issue of my return to school has not been raised. The thought fills me with dread. We are living in a state of limbo, between two lives. The life we had with Mum and the one we will have without her. For now, time stands still. Once I am back at school, that new life will start. There will be no going back, ever.

The idea of staying cocooned here forever is extremely appealing, however, I need to be realistic. The more school I miss, the further behind I will get, and the harder I will have to work to catch up. The thought of all that work is terrifying, as is the very real fear that the craziness might start up again. All those people I might touch. Thinking about it makes me feel ill.

Sophie, Georgie and Izzy have called regularly. I let their calls go through to the answering machine. It is nice to hear their voices, to know that they are there for me, but I feel no need to talk. What is there to say?

Since Rosie moved to Greenfields, on her good days, she calls every night after the evening news, right on six thirty. She has called every day since the funeral. It is unusual for her to have more than three consecutive good days. She often has three or four bad days in a row. For now at least her grief is winning over her dementia. I don't know if that is a good thing for her. It certainly has been for me. The sound of her voice on the phone is an anchor, grounding me.

I have not touched my laptop. I have no desire to. For once I don't envy my friend's iPhones and Blackberries. I am embracing my isolation.

There are no rules for how to behave when something like this happens. Dad and I seem to be in synch with each other. We are both content here, in the home that was ours with Mum, and is now ours alone. People understand.

Someone has organised things so that each evening a meal is delivered to our front door. A brief knock on the first night startled me so much it took some time before I responded. When I got to the door, nobody was there. Just a covered dish containing a mushroom risotto, a note attached telling us to leave the dish on the doorstep once we were done.

Dad opens his eyes. In that waking moment, before he plasters his face with a smile, he looks immensely sad. The guilt becomes a scalding, searing ache inside me. Will I ever see him smile out of pure happiness again? Do I deserve to?

We pass the day as we have the last few, quietly sharing our meals and occasionally listening to the radio. We sleep whenever the need arises, which is far more often than I thought possible. Sleep is like a drug. The more I have, the more I want.

Tomorrow is Sunday, the day we ritually visit Rosie. When she calls at 6:30, she tells Dad she doesn't expect us to come. Looking at me as he speaks, Dad tells her we will definitely be there. I nod eagerly in agreement. Rosie is the closest connection I have to Lily. I look forward to seeing her so much, I almost feel upbeat. Here's hoping she can repel her demons for one more day.

# Chapter 10

Mum and I are walking in a green field dotted with tiny white flowers. She is wearing a beautiful, long, flowing, white dress. Her feet are bare. Her hair is loose and shining in the sun. We are walking side by side, our footfalls perfectly matched. A gentle breeze blows.

Looking up I notice Mum is now a few paces ahead of me. I increase my pace a little to keep up but don't seem to be making any ground. I call to her to slow down, to wait for me. I start to walk faster still. She looks back at me over her shoulder, her face wearing that captivating smile but she doesn't wait. I am trotting. Her smiling face is still ahead of me, further away. I am running now. I can't bridge the distance between us.

My alarm goes off waking me with a jolt. Reality, an enormous wave, crashes over me, leaving me gasping for air. The tears come hot and fast and I surrender to them.

Mum firmly believed breakfast set the tone for the day. We always ate a proper meal together. Whether waffles or bacon and eggs, there was always coffee brewing, freshly squeezed juice, and background music playing. Dad is trying so hard to fill the gaping void. It brings tears to my eyes. He has attempted pancakes. They lie limply on a plate on the kitchen bench. Thanking him, I give him the biggest smile I am capable of. Placing two pancakes on my plate, I smother them in maple syrup. The mass in my stomach still takes up most of the available room. I eat what I can with feigned enthusiasm. It seems to please him, which is all that matters.

During the drive to Greenfields, Dad plays one of Mum's favourite CDs, just as he would if she were here. He sings a phrase or two, sometimes a whole chorus, clearly doing his best to keep the mood light. With great difficulty I manage to sing a chorus, but the tears are so close I have to stop.

Rosie is waiting in reception. I can instantly tell today is a good day. I had no idea how much I was dreading finding Rosie away with the fairies until the relief at seeing her well surges through me. For the first time I am struck by the similarity between her and Mum. They have the same eyes and the same radiant smile. I hug her, hesitantly at first, in case the madness starts up again. When nothing happens, I give her a proper hug. She has her own special smell, sweet but not cloying, flowery but not too strong. I wish I could bottle it.

The weather is perfect so we walk in the garden. Rosie is chatty, keeping us entertained with stories from her youth. She grew up, the fifth of six children, all girls except the baby, Fred. Some of these anecdotes I have heard before. It is nice not having to think. Her voice washes over me as she recalls tale upon tale.

Eventually, tired of walking, we sit. Rosie and Dad on a bench, me on the grass by Rosie's feet, holding her hand. Rosie relates another story. She squeezes my hand softly but firmly, refocusing my attention, cleverly warning me to listen without alerting Dad.

"Not long after I was born, my eldest sister Frances became unwell. I don't know what caused the illness, but she nearly died. She was sick for weeks. My parents nursed her through it, keeping vigil by her bedside. Once she recovered, she discovered the illness had left her with a surprising talent."

At this, she clasps my hand a little tighter before continuing.

"Frances only had to hold your hand to tell you everything you had in your pockets, or anywhere else on your body. It was a wonderful party trick, but a terrible nuisance if you had something you shouldn't."

A current passes between us. I look to Dad expecting him to have noticed something. He is oblivious. The faraway look in his eyes makes me wonder if he has heard Rosie's story at all. Rosie continues with her narrative.

"Our mother, your great-grandmother Ava, explained that it was what her family called the 'Gift'. The Gift ran only in the women of the family, often skipping a generation as it had in her case. It rarely took the same form. She told us that her mother Mary could divine the gender of an unborn child by placing her hands on the belly of a pregnant woman, no matter how early in the pregnancy. Mary's sister Ruby, could tell you everything you had eaten in the last day just by holding your hand."

Now looking directly at me she says, "I was always so envious of Frances, wishing it had been me who had the Gift."

Is Rosie trying to tell me I have the Gift? The word conjures up images of beautifully wrapped, beribboned packages, not horrifying hallucinations like the ones I have experienced. I have so many questions. I don't want to make Dad suspicious, so sticking to the most burning ones, I try to keep the urgency out of my voice.

"Did the Gift always come after an illness?"

"Well, that's an interesting question, Juno," replies Rosie. "Mary's Gift started after she had her first baby. Apparently, it was a difficult birth, probably quite traumatic, but in those days most births were. I have no idea when Ruby's Gift began."

I continue to keep my voice level, trying in vain to conceal the hope I feel as I ask, "Did the Gift last forever or did it only last for a while?"

Rosie smiles sadly as she explains, "Frances died aged twenty-six from polio, but she had the Gift until then."

Sounding brighter, she adds, "My grandmother Mary told me Lily would be a girl only months before she passed away aged seventy-four."

At the mention of Mum's name, Dad's attention is back with us. When he speaks it is nothing to do with what we have been discussing.

"Almost lunch time, shall we go in?"

Sunday is family day at Greenfields. They always put on a roast lunch for residents and their visitors. There are enough people at lunch for me not to have to talk. My head is filled with questions about what I've just learnt. Did Mum know about the Gift? Did anyone who had it ever work out how to turn it off, using it only when they wanted? It is hard for me to see the Gift as anything other than punishment for my selfish behaviour. As far as retribution goes it is exceedingly effective.

After lunch, Rosie announces she is tired. She often does this. Mum once said she thought it was Rosie's way of helping us leave without feeling guilty. Sometimes we ignore her, staying on in the garden to enjoy the afternoon sun. Today, Dad doesn't argue. I still have unanswered questions, but they will have to wait.

Walking with us towards the car, Rosie broaches the subject of school. Without hesitation, I explain that I have decided to return tomorrow. Dad looks at me in surprise. The look is soon gone and he seems relieved, in a sad resigned way. The weight of what has happened hovers over us.

At home, we are met by the pungent odour of dying flowers. I collect the vases one by one, taking them into the kitchen. Disposing of the wilting blooms sent to commemorate Mum feels like a betrayal. It is also cathartic. With this action, I am taking the step that will drag both Dad and I over the border, between the sheltered life we have been living, and the daunting time that stretches endlessly ahead.

# Chapter 11

My alarm is set for 6:30am. I switch it off at 6:20. I have been lying awake since 4:23. When I had all the time in the world to sleep, it was all I did. Now that my time to sleep is limited, it is no longer possible. I have spent the time thinking. I can't turn back the clock but I can convince Dad I am fine. This will allow him to focus on his healing, rather than wasting precious time and energy worrying about me.

Crying in the shower alleviates the worry of Dad hearing me. When I get to the kitchen, Dad is already there, smiling as he hands me a plate bearing a watery omelette.

"How are you feeling about school today?"

I notice he is not wearing a suit. Clearly he isn't planning a return to work yet.

"A little nervous. I'll be fine once I get there." My voice sounds far more confident than I feel.

"I thought I'd drive you in …?" This is a statement with a hint of a question mark at the end.

"That's ok, Dad. It's probably best if I go on the bus as usual."

He takes a little persuading, finally agreeing to let me go alone. He reassures me that if during the day I find it all too much, I only need call him, and he will collect me. Before I walk out the door, we give each other a hug. I am relieved, feeling nothing other than his arms around me. Perhaps the craziness is over. Maybe I never had the Gift at all.

I hope to make my arrival at school as low-key as possible. As much as I love Sophie and the others, right now I would give anything to be the only person on the planet. The idea of hiding away at home forever is very appealing. This is so unlike me that even I can't understand it. How will I explain it to others? I haven't told anyone I am coming and arrive at my stop just in time for the late bus. Normally Sophie and I meet on the early bus, she gets on one stop after me. I have no reason to think she will be on this bus today. Once on, I quickly scan each row. I see a few faces I recognise from school, dotted amongst the general commuters, but nobody I know well. Walking past them, it's impossible to miss the dawning in their eyes as they realise it's me, the girl whose mother just died. Lowering my gaze, I move quickly down the aisle, sitting in the first empty row I come to.

I breathe a sigh of relief when we pass Sophie's stop and she isn't there. Two stops later, Jamie Eaton gets on. He is several years below me at school and his mother Kerrie was an old school friend of Mum's. She also happens to be my chemistry teacher. I remember how pleased Mum was when we found out I was going to be in one of Kerrie's classes. Occasionally our families get together at weekends, so Jamie knows me. He is a beautiful-looking child. Soft, blonde curls frame his heart-shaped face. He has widely set, big, blue eyes and a small perfectly shaped nose. His lips are full and the dimple on his chin adds to his look of innocence. He is a very sweet boy, suffering mildly from Asperger Syndrome. He tends to be a lot more interesting than other kids his age.

I can't help wondering why he is even taking the bus to school. Surely he could get a ride with his mother? I look away before our eyes meet, hoping to discourage him from sitting next to me. I gaze fixedly out the window, repeating the mantra, 'Do not sit next to me! Do not sit next to me,' over and over in my mind. Sadly it doesn't work. Lacking spatial awareness, he almost sits in my lap. My head starts to spin. The lights go out…

Now, I am in a brightly lit room, one I have been in before. It is a tastefully renovated, open-plan kitchen, the kind you might see gracing the pages of a glossy magazine. The space is beautiful, but the atmosphere is ugly. Kerrie stands at the sink, her back to the room. I am sitting at a table, a bowl of cereal in front of me, slowly spooning it into my mouth. On my left sits Kerrie's husband Brian, wearing a suit and drinking coffee. Suddenly Kerrie is yelling.

"How do I know you're telling me the truth? How do you expect me to trust you after what happened, after the *years* of lies?"

A child starts crying loudly. Only now do I notice Jamie's younger sister Giselle sitting on my right.

"You're not going to bring that all up again are you? Haven't we been through this enough? How long are you going to punish me for one mistake?"

The exasperation in his voice is barely concealed. Kerrie grabs a towel, drying her hands as she moves towards the now screaming Giselle.

Her voice catches as she says, "One mistake that lasted *six* months! How do you expect me to believe you when you tell me that you are planning to go on this trip alone?"

"Kerrie, trust me, I'm doing this for our future. It's a huge deal." His tone is pleading.

"One that could be great for us, if I can just get it over the line. This trip to the States may just be the thing that clinches it."

Kerrie turns away. Walking out of the room, Giselle perched on her hip, she looks back over her shoulder to deliver her parting comment.

"It may just be the thing that finishes us!"...

I am back on the bus. While I am horrified to discover the Gift is still with me, I feel enormously sad for Jamie. I have witnessed a handful of fights between my parents but none as awful as the one I just saw. I always imagined if my parents fought, they did it in private, not wanting to upset me. I wonder if Mum knew what Kerrie was going through.

Jamie is looking at me. I wonder what it looks like from the outside when I am having one of my turns. The look on his face is expectant; he is waiting for me to say something. I smile at him hoping that is enough to satisfy him.

"It's ok if you don't want to talk about it. I guess you must be really sad and I know it's sometimes really hard to talk when

58

you're really upset about something. Once, when my turtle Norbert died, I didn't speak to anyone for two whole days."

Nothing makes me cry more than kindness. Why is that? People can be so nasty, and that makes me angry. When somebody is unexpectedly kind to me, I immediately feel like crying. The tears start to come. I force them away. Thinking about the phone call I made that ended my mother's life does it. I turn back to Jamie, a small smile on my lips, hoping to show him he is right, I am too sad to talk. He seems to understand.

We sit in silence the rest of the way to school. I try not to touch him again. His body bumps into mine a couple of times as the bus rounds corners. Each time, I tense up, steeling myself against what might happen. Nothing does, which I am thankful for. It appears that once I have touched somebody and had an experience, I can touch them soon after, and feel nothing at all. If this is how it works it will definitely make living with the Gift easier.

# Chapter 12

Finally, we arrive at school. I wait for Jamie and the other students to get off the bus before I stand, scared of touching someone. I am tempted to stay on the bus and just go home but this will only worry Dad. The bus stop is only metres away from the school's main entrance. Inside the gates, there is a steep hill to negotiate, after which you come to a covered walkway, that leads past the science labs, into the main square. In the far right corner of the square sits the reception and Mr. Fitzgerald's offices. Paved walkways branch off from each side of the square to different parts of the school.

Each morning, I normally take the right-hand path, leading to the playing fields, and beyond that to the drama theatre, art and music rooms. Most mornings we congregate on the fields, catching up on anything important that has transpired in the intervening hours since we were last together. You would imagine that nightly phone calls and Skype sessions would reduce the amount we have to say to each other every morning. The opposite seems to be true.

This morning is anything but normal. Today I turn in the opposite direction, towards the library and main school building. My plan is to go straight to my locker, then to biology before the bell rings, minimising the chance of bumping into people. Sophie is in my biology class. There is no way I can get through a class without us touching. I need to be sitting down when she arrives. I am so busy strategising, it takes me a while to realise I am the centre of attention. Clusters of students have slowed, in some cases even stopped. They look at me with a mixture of curiosity, sadness and pity.

People who have never noticed me before are looking at me with genuine interest and concern. Even students who I have never had anything to do with are smiling sadly at me. This is crazy. Normally I move in this world unnoticed, hoping to be seen. Everything is upended. For the first time I want to be invisible; disturbingly, I am more visible than ever.

Walking towards my locker, I keep my head slightly bowed. I retrieve my biology books before continuing straight to the lab. I sense people whispering all around me, wherever I go. I watch in amazement as they move out of my path. It is a surreal experience but at least I don't need to worry about being jostled by people.

I am in my usual seat when the bell rings. My classmates enter, chatting and laughing – until they notice me. This renders them mute. Most immediately look away. Some look at me. Some smile sadly, shyly; others acknowledge me with a sombre nod.

Sophie is so taken aback at seeing me, she actually comes to a halt, standing stock-still in the middle of the room. I know her so well, I can virtually read her thoughts. Her face registers hurt, because I didn't tell her I planned to return today. This lasts so briefly that, to the uninitiated, it would have gone unnoticed. The smile she gives me after is so warm and full of feeling, I have to fight back tears. She approaches slowly, sits next to me, reaches for my hand and takes it in both of hers.

I am prepared this time. The giddiness and darkness have little impact, both lasting only briefly…

I am in a park I know well. It is the one Sophie and I often meet in, as it lies about halfway between our homes. Sophie's younger siblings, Teya and Eliot are on the swings. I, or should I say Sophie, is pushing Eliot's swing. I recognise the shirt on the arms that for now belong to me as one of Sophie's favourites.

"Higher!" screams Eliot, "Higher, higher!"

"My turn!" yells Teya.

Sophie gives Eliot's seat a mighty shove before walking over to push Teya. Just as Eliot's swing reaches the highest point, he lets go of both chains, flying off the seat. Time slows down. Eliot's tiny body floats in mid-air. Time returns to normal speed. His arms and legs flail uselessly, unable to stop his body slamming into the earth…

I am back in the lab. The teacher stands at the front of the class. He is looking at me, his face a mask of concern. I smile to help allay his fears. He gives me a relieved smile in return.

"Are you feeling alright, Juno?"

I nod nervously, worried how my voice might sound, my nerves still reacting to the scene I just witnessed.

"Welcome back," he continues, "I am sure that I speak for everyone in the class when I say how sorry and saddened we were to hear of your mother's passing."

I nod again but say nothing, anxious not to prolong the one-sided conversation. He turns his attention back to the class as he begins the lesson on reproduction and inheritance.

I need to ask Sophie about Eliot. Some classes make chatting to each other easy. This is not one of them. I am comforted by the thought that if something really terrible had happened, Sophie wouldn't be here now. She seems happy enough, so hopefully he is just fine. As soon as the bell rings, I ask as casually as I can how Teya and Eliot are.

"They're good. Eliot had an accident in the park. He was concussed, but he's back to normal now, and driving us all crazy again."

This is said with a smile, and a rueful laugh, which only hints at how traumatic the incident had been. I don't press her for details. I already have them. As we stand, she moves to link her arm through mine. I brace myself just in case. Nothing happens.

Together we walk down the corridor. News of my return to school seems to have spread. Those who didn't see me earlier are having a good look now. Occasionally, I bump briefly into somebody and feel momentarily woozy, but as soon as the contact stops, so does the light-headedness.

My next lesson is maths. Thankfully, none of the others are in my class, and I feel myself relax. As Sophie and I part ways, she calls over her shoulder.

"See you at break?"

This would not normally be a question. I nod half-heartedly. Thinking about touching the others, like Izzy and Georgie, terrifies me.

I make my way to class, taking a seat in the empty back row. I choose the desk farthest to the right. My classmates file in and stop talking as they register my presence. Nobody sits next to me. Perhaps they are worried my grief is contagious. I expect a condolence speech from my maths teacher. Instead, she smiles at me warmly.

"Juno, while you were away…" She is interrupted mid-sentence as the door opens, and a boy I have never seen before enters the room. He is very tall and slim with brown hair.

"Ah, you must be Toby. Welcome to Edgecliff High." At this the boy nods and smiles at us all.

"Everybody, this is Toby Moxham - he has just moved into the area. Please make him welcome."

It feels good to be staring rather than being stared at. This thought makes me feel guilty, so I look away. There are a few empty seats but, perhaps motivated by the same reasons as me, Toby moves towards the back row, and sits next to me.

"As I was saying, we have begun work on trigonometry," she continues pointedly looking in our direction.

"So Juno, Toby, if today's lesson makes little sense, don't worry, I'll help the two of you catch up."

Toby looks at me, smiles and winks conspiratorially. I smile back. He must think I am a new student too. His smile is warm and genuine. For as long as that smile lasts, I feel good. Here is somebody that doesn't know me as the girl whose Mum just died.

Once I move my gaze to the whiteboard, to the equations projected there, this feeling vanishes. I have only been gone a week. Looking at those equations, it would be possible to imagine I have been gone a year. Thinking back over the last week only strengthens this feeling. How can my life have changed so dramatically in the space of one week?

It takes all my concentration to follow the lesson. I am left with no time for worrying about anything else. When the bell goes the teacher asks Toby and I to stay behind. Toby tells her that he covered trigonometry at his old school. I explain that I think I understood most of it but will work through the chapter in the text book, letting her know if I am still unclear about anything.

As we leave the classroom, Toby opens the door for me, something that only my father has ever done.

"I can help you with trig if you need. Just let me know."

I thank him. There's that smile again. I can feel my cheeks warming. I am sure they are glowing red.

"There you are!" shrieks Georgie, bounding towards us, but the sight of Toby next to me stops her in her tracks.

"Oh! Who's this then?" she asks.

"Toby, this is Georgie, George, this is Toby. Toby just started at school today."

Now it's Toby's turn to look puzzled. Until a moment ago, he assumed I was new to the school too.

"I'll explain later, I promise," I offer, turning to him with an apologetic look.

"Welcome Toby!" sings Georgie, as she links her arm with mine. She leans in to whisper in my ear, but I hear nothing...

It's happening again. My vision disappears so briefly it is almost unnoticeable. I am walking along a path towards my own front door, my arm linked through someone else's. I let go of my companion's arm as she takes a key from her pocket, inserting it into the lock. She opens the door, walking in ahead of me. I am looking at myself. We are chatting and giggling. We walk down the hallway past my bedroom door, turning right into the lounge, on our way to the kitchen. As we walk through the living room, I see my father sitting on the sofa. He is cleanly shaven, wearing a suit. Despite this, he still looks awful. He's been crying. With a jolt, I realise what I am seeing.

"Juno, Georgie," he says, "Come - please sit down. I have something to tell you."

I try desperately to talk, to say something. I try to tell him I already know. He doesn't have to go through this again. But it is useless. I am merely a passive witness. I have no power to direct the action. I have to stand and watch this scene play out, just as Georgie had such a short time ago.

"Dad, you're scaring me, what is it?" The voice next to me, my voice, sounds so small and so terrified.

"I'm so sorry, darling. There's been an accident. It's Lily."

He is desperately fighting back tears but losing the battle. Through Georgie's eyes, I watch myself jump up off the sofa.

"What is it, Dad? What's happened? Is she ok? Where is she?"

The words pour out of me. He reaches for my hands, holding them in his as he says softly,

"Juno, sweetheart, I'm so, so, sorry. It's Lily... She's gone. She's ... gone."

I watch as my body slumps to the floor. My father leans over me. He calls my name softly, tenderly stroking my face. Weeping, he lifts my shoulders, shaking me, gently at first, then with increasing vigour. Hysterically sobbing my name over and over, louder and louder.

"Georgie," he cries looking up at me, "Call an ambulance! Quickly!"...

"Juno?" I am in the hallway at school. Georgie looks frantic.

"Are you ok? What happened? Do you have a headache? Do you need water? Shall we go to the nurse? Do you want to go home? I can take you. Do you want me to call your dad?"

I am still standing - which is a plus. This may have something to do with the fact that Georgie has a vice-like grip on both my upper arms. I reassure her that I am fine. She reluctantly releases her hold on me. I feel utterly drained.

"What just happened? I was so scared. I thought you were going to faint again. Are you sure you're ok?"

Poor Georgie. Witnessing that scene firsthand must have been traumatic.

"There's nothing to worry about, I just get a little dizzy now and again." This isn't a lie. "The doctor says it's not unusual given what happened." This is, but I'd say anything right now to help Georgie calm down.

She visibly relaxes, giving me an enormous hug. I instantly stiffen. Nothing happens so I hug her back. The scene I have just relived comes back at me with full force. I am crying now. Georgie is too. This is the first time she has had an opportunity to grieve with me. I have been so consumed by my own suffering and guilt, I failed to consider how much my mother's death had impacted those close to me.

Georgie and I manage to stop crying and pull apart. I notice Toby. He is watching us with a mixture of concern and bewilderment. I can't begin to imagine what he is thinking. He probably thinks I am totally crazy. He isn't the only one. I try to smile convincingly at him. I have no idea how that actually translates on my tear-streaked face. It seems to work. His expression softens. He looks slightly if not totally relieved although his confusion is still evident.

Georgie links one arm with mine, the other with Toby's. He looks a little startled. Georgie is totally unaware. She has begun a steady stream of chatter about Edgecliff High. I am pleased Toby is distracted. I owe him an explanation but I don't have the energy for that right now. Georgie is steering us to the playing fields. Weather permitting, this is our usual meeting place for break and lunch. Everyone is powerless against Georgie once she has made up her mind. It seems she has decided Toby is joining us.

# Chapter 13

Sophie and Izzy are already sitting under the Moreton Bay fig tree, by the side of the field. I am determined to avoid touching Izzy. I don't think I can stand another experience right now. I sit as far away from her as possible. Our eyes meet. I can see she is hurt and uncertain. I look away, unable for the moment to do anything more. Poor Izzy. I didn't take her call last week; today she must think I am avoiding her. This is the first time I have seen her since Lily's accident. I understand she is grieving too. I feel bad for her, but guilt is an emotion I am fast learning to live with. Thankfully, Toby's presence helps to distract us all. Georgie performs the introductions before announcing,

"These are the girls! You'll meet the boys at lunch."

Georgie and Izzy start peppering Toby with questions. As he volleys back answers good-naturedly, his story begins to emerge. His father is an Inspector in the police force. He has been transferred here from Richmond in Melbourne. He is sixteen, turning seventeen on January 23$^{rd}$, making him an Aquarian. This pleases Sophie.

His favourite sport is cricket, but he also plays rugby. He plays the saxophone. His best subject is maths. He likes most animals but is not a big fan of cats. His preferred type of music is jazz.

Georgie then asks Toby which teachers he has been assigned. He pulls out his timetable and she pores over it, telling him which classes he shares with each of us, critiquing the teachers as she goes.

"Oh you're so lucky, you have Mr. Lennox for drama! Izzy and Juno do too. He is the best teacher in the whole school."

Sophie is yet to participate in the interrogation, but has taken everything in. She gets to the heart of things very quickly. In her gentle voice she says,

"You mentioned your father's transfer. Is it just the two of you?"

Unlike his other answers, this one seems to require some thought. Toby looks at Sophie. For the briefest moment, he seems sad. Perhaps it's just me projecting my own emotions onto him. Lowering his eyes, he answers yes, before deftly turning the spotlight onto me.

"What about you, Juno? Where have you been? Why are you starting back at school today?"

I have never been happier to hear the bell ring. I am sure I sense relief amongst the others too. I jump up, grab my bag, calling over my shoulder as I leave,

"I have to go to double English. Mrs. Samuels goes ballistic if we're late. See you all at lunch."

Sophie, Georgie, Izzy, her twin Oliver and Jasper are all in the same English class. Two weeks ago, I would have given my right arm to be

70

with them. Today, I feel enormously relieved not to be. I am the first student in the room. Mrs. Samuels is at her desk reading. I decide to try a new tactic. I sit in the front row. Mrs. Samuels looks up. She starts to tell me how sorry she is. The doors are thrown open. The rest of the class pours in. Her condolence is cut short. We both know what was intended.

Many of my fellow students have seen me by now. Noticing me again causes only a small reduction in the noise level. I am sure in a couple of days, seeing me in a class will produce no effect at all. On the one hand, this thought pleases me. On the other, it seems incredibly wrong that within a fortnight of Lily's passing, to so many people, it will be as though she never died. Their lives will carry on, almost as though she never lived to begin with.

Mrs. Samuels tells us all to get out our copies of *Great Expectations*. She explains that during the week I was away, they covered the chapter where Pip's sister, known as Mrs. Joe, is viciously attacked, following which she becomes invalided and mute. *Great Expectations* was one of Mum's favourite books. This is probably my fourth time reading it. I don't feel at all out of my depth.

Mrs. Samuels is an extraordinary teacher. It is actually possible to lose yourself in one of her classes. Before I know it, the bell is ringing and everyone is filing off to their next class. To avoid touching anyone, I wait until most people have left before standing. I make my way to my history class. Although the sea is not parting the way it did earlier, people are still aware of me, doing their best to avoid touching me. Under other circumstances this would make me feel like a leper.

None of the girls are in my history class but Ollie and his friend Ben are. Thankfully, the desks are in pairs and the boys always sit together. It would be hard to imagine twins looking more different than Izzy and Ollie do. Where Izzy is fair-haired and blue-eyed, Ollie is dark-haired with green eyes. Izzy's skin is lily-white; Ollie's is olive.

71

The differences are not just superficial either. Izzy has trouble catching a ball. Ollie makes the A team in every sport he ever tries out for. Even stranger, Ollie is left-handed and Izzy right.

Ollie is already seated next to Ben. When he sees me, he grins hugely at me. On anyone else this would seem the strangest behaviour under the circumstances. From Ollie, it is totally natural. On that score at least, Izzy and Ollie are exactly the same. They both have huge hearts. Ben shoots me a half smile. I can see he is struggling, wondering how to behave around me. I have no idea how I would act if I were in his place, so I empathise.

There are no spare seats near Ollie and Ben so I sit at the first empty pair of desks I find. Piper Reid sits next to me. We have been in the same three history lessons each week since the beginning of this year, but barely know each other. Piper has thick, straight, red hair that she habitually wears in a plait wound into a bun. Her fair skin has a smattering of freckles concentrated mainly around her nose. Her eyes are a dark green. She is probably the tallest girl in the year, yet wears her uniform longer than anyone else. I know nothing at all about her, except that she moved to our school at the beginning of this year. Georgie has loads of classes with her. She has tried on several occasions to strike up a conversation, but each time, Piper has shut her down, which is no mean feat. She keeps very much to herself, so I can relax and pay attention to the lesson.

The teacher, Mr. Hardy, is the last person in. Scanning the room until he finds me, he starts to speak. The condolence speech sounds prepared. Before long he has moved on from me and is telling us about his own mother's passing when he was twenty-three. This hardly seems relevant, but means that I am no longer the centre of attention.

Finally, the lecture is over and we begin the lesson about Australia's involvement in World War II. This class requires so little student involvement that it is hard to stay focused. I soon find my attention drifting to the problem of touching Izzy. I need to get it over with. I can already feel her beginning to get paranoid. I really don't want to hurt her feelings any more than I have. I devise a plan I will put into action at lunch. With that done, I tune back in to the lesson.

My plan means I need to get to the playing field quickly. I surreptitiously pack my bag ahead of time. As soon as the bell goes, I am up and out the door without even a backward glance at Ollie and Ben. It is unlike me, but I feel certain any unusual behaviour today will be forgiven. I am the first one to arrive, but out of the corner of my eye, I see Sophie and Toby are walking towards me. I remove my sandwich from my bag, feigning interest in it. One look at Toby tells me he is now in possession of all the facts. Gone is the playful smile he wore this morning, replaced with the same sad, apologetic one I have seen on countless faces.

Thankfully, Georgie and Izzy arrive minutes later, shattering the awkward silence. Izzy makes straight for me. As she sits, I execute my plan. Placing my uneaten sandwich down, I take my head in both hands, groaning audibly. Everyone is immediately concerned. I feel slightly remorseful but not enough to stop me going ahead.

"It's ok, I just have a bit of a headache."

Still holding my head, I close my eyes, turn and lay my head in Izzy's lap…

Instantly I am back in the Crematorium. I am sitting about five rows from the front on the right-hand side of the room. Izzy's hand is being held tightly by someone who I am fairly certain is Ollie, although her gaze is trained squarely ahead. In her free hand she is clutching a ball of tissues. The dark red wood coffin stands alone at the front of the room. I can see the back of my head in the front row, sandwiched between Rosie's and Dad's. Izzy's hand lifts to swipe the already sodden tissues ineffectively at the tears coursing down her cheeks. As Josh Groban's *To Where You Are* starts to play, the curtains begin to move towards each other. I watch once more as the coffin containing my mother, slides backwards and disappears, forever…

My head is still in Izzy's lap. She looks anxiously into my eyes. I smile up at her. The worry fades from her face. I promise her that I am fine, that in fact my headache has gone. I sit up, aware that everyone is looking at me. I pretend not to notice as I pick up my sandwich and carry on eating. Despite what I have just witnessed, I experience a strange sense of calm. Perhaps it is because now that I have touched all three girls, I have effectively rendered them safe.

Ollie, Jasper and Ben arrive noisily. Jasper plonks himself down next to Izzy. Without any preamble, he tells me how sorry he is about Mum. It is said with ease and sincerity. I gratefully accept his condolences, enormously relieved that the boys aren't inclined to hug me.

Georgie introduces Toby to Ollie, Jasper and Ben. She explains that Ollie is Izzy's twin, and Jasper is Izzy's boyfriend. Jasper and Izzy have been together for close to two years. It's hard to imagine a more compatible couple. The boys start talking to Toby so I am out of the limelight. The boys' questions centre around sport as they determine which teams Toby barracks for in each of the different codes. Not surprisingly, there is no mention of star-signs. Before long, they are up and playing soccer. Watching them, it is hard to believe this is Toby's first day here.

Our usually very chatty group is awkwardly silent today. The loss of my mother hangs in the air around me like a dark cloud, infecting anyone who comes too near. Finally, Georgie breaks the silence. It seems she has decided the best way forward is to act as normal as possible.

"He's very cute," she says with a smile in my direction.

This is clearly an assessment of Toby, aimed at me. Perhaps being the one who met him first means that I will be held responsible for his strengths and shortcomings. I smile, shrugging my shoulders noncommittally. He is cute, but I have enough on my mind without adding anything or anyone else into the mix.

The look Sophie gives me shows she is uncertain about Georgie's tactics. She wants to be sure that senseless chatter is not upsetting me. I do my best to show her I am fine. Whether this is true or not is something not even I know. It feels wrong sitting here in the sunshine talking about boys less than a week after Mum's funeral, but would I rather we were all here crying?

The girls continue to talk through Toby's merits. I am suddenly so exhausted, all I want to do is sleep. Using my bag as a pillow, I lay down on the grass. This feels like the longest day I have ever lived through - and it's not over yet. I doze off and am woken by the bell.

Sophie and I both have chemistry now and we go straight to class together. I am not looking forward to seeing Kerrie Eaton, but we are greeted by a substitute teacher who informs us that Mrs. Eaton is absent today. I fleetingly wonder whether her absence has anything to do with what I saw this morning.

The substitute teacher knows nothing about any of us so I am free to be a regular student for this period at least. We are given a worksheet on metals. I try to concentrate but am so tired it is a huge struggle. I have double P.E. next. The thought of physical exercise right now actually makes me feel nauseous. I make a decision to skip it and go home early, which instantly helps me to feel a little better.

Once the bell has stopped ringing, I tell Sophie what I have decided to do. She hugs me goodbye, promising to call me tonight. I tell her I am wiped out and will be in bed early. As always, she understands. I wait at the bus stop. When the bus arrives it is almost empty. I find a seat next to the window placing my bag on the seat next to mine to discourage anyone from sitting there.

I go over each of the episodes I have had, trying to work out the things they have in common. They always happen when someone touches me. I always witness an event that is terrifying, stressful, or terribly sad. The events seem to be recent ones – although I can't be sure when Jamie Eaton witnessed the argument between his parents. That fight could have happened months ago, but something tells me this is not the case. As far as I can tell, I haven't touched anyone for the first time since I fainted, and not had an experience. Why is it that everyone I touch has had a horribly stressful event in his or her recent past? Is it just bad luck? What would happen if I touched somebody who hasn't? The most positive thing is, once I have seen someone's memory, I can safely touch them again.

I arrive home to an empty house, a not quite thawed homemade chicken pie on the front doorstep, complete with cooking instructions. I am going through my trigonometry when Dad arrives home. I don't ask where he's been, thankful that he doesn't know I skipped the last two periods. It would only make him worry.

I am so desperate to speak to Rosie that I must have glanced at the clock a hundred times between 6:00 and 6:30. When the call finally comes, I allow Dad to answer it. After he has finished speaking with her, he passes the phone to me. For me to desire privacy during a phone conversation with Rosie would be unusual. However, Dad is currently preoccupied with paperwork, allowing me to take the phone into my room without arousing any suspicion.

Rosie is very eager to continue our conversation from yesterday. I tell her about every vision I have had since I woke up in hospital. It feels so good to be able to tell somebody without fear of being judged utterly insane. Normally, Mum is the one I would turn to with any problems that are too big for me to handle alone. Now that she is gone, Rosie is my next stop. I am so grateful that she has managed to ward off her illness for as long as she has.

Having heard everything I have to say, Rosie is insistent that I have the Gift and that in time I will learn to manage it, perhaps even welcome it. She is very empathetic, understanding my fear, but it is impossible for her to disguise her underlying excitement. I wish I felt the same. She tells me she loves me and I tell her I love her more to which she replies, "Impossible."

This is our standard telephone goodbye. It usually makes me smile. Tonight, it brings tears to my eyes. I go to bed feeling much lighter. Opening up to Rosie has somehow relieved me a little of the burden I have been carrying. I am so exhausted that nothing can keep me awake.

# Chapter 14

I open my eyes. It is 5:19. Rather than lie here trying to go back to sleep, I decide to put the time to good use. I do some trigonometry practice before getting ready. By the time Dad arrives in the kitchen, there is a plate of bacon, eggs and toast waiting for him. He is so pleased that I wonder why I haven't thought about doing this sooner? Perhaps the fog left behind from the stupor is finally beginning to lift. My stone stomach, as I have begun to think of it, has not shifted, yet I make an effort to eat the breakfast I have prepared.

The apprehension I felt yesterday has all but disappeared. I am absolutely certain that today is going to be a far easier one. I decide to take the early bus, as sitting next to Sophie has got to be safer than sitting next to a total stranger.

I sit in our usual spot in the third row when I get on the bus, saving the seat next to me for Sophie. When she sits down, I am prepared, just in case touching her sends me off again, but nothing happens. She asks me how I'm doing. I tell her that it's hard but I'm doing all right, all things considered. Sophie lacks Georgie's ability to carry on as though everything is the same. Instead, she takes my hand in hers. We travel to school mostly in silence. This suits me just fine.

As I make my way around the school, I notice some people go out of their way to avoid looking at me. Others make a point of acknowledging me, at the same time recognising my grief. I understand those that don't want to meet my eye, don't want to dip, however briefly, into my pain. I appreciate those brave enough to do so.

When I enter the room for maths, Toby is sitting in the same seat as yesterday. He smiles as soon as he sees me. I take the seat next to him. He needlessly apologises for misunderstanding my situation yesterday. It is hardly his fault. I make sure he knows this. I change the subject, asking him a question I have about trig. He patiently talks me through it until the class begins.

After class, Toby explains he won't see me until lunch, as he has a meeting with the head of the sports department during break. Clearly, where he spends his break is not my business, but I am pleased that he thinks it might be.

Ollie is in my physics class. I am careful to get there early. I sit in the back corner rather than where we normally sit. The teacher barely acknowledges my presence. I earn a slight nod of the head as she looks at me over the top of her glasses, perched precariously on the tip of her nose. Part of me is pleased at having to escape another sympathy speech. Part of me is angry she doesn't feel the need to do more.

When she begins the lesson, I am relieved to discover that we are still on the broad topic of Space. We are now looking at the present understanding about its relationship with time, and how this has been dependent upon earlier models of the transmission of light. It is difficult enough to warrant my full attention. I gladly give it, leaving no time or room for other thoughts.

I keep my head buried in my book after the bell, to avoid having to walk with Ollie. I am the last to leave the room. The teacher takes the opportunity to approach me. She doesn't move to touch me, thankfully, but tells me she is terribly sorry to hear about what happened. She asks me to let her know if I need any extra help with physics, or just someone to talk to. I am truly grateful for the speech, not least because it didn't happen in front of an audience.

I am the last to arrive on the lawn for lunch. Everyone is there, including Toby. I ask how his meeting went. He explains that he will be joining the rugby training sessions from now on, and will be slotted into a team once they see how he plays. This news is greeted by whoops and claps on the back from the other boys. Soon they are all up and playing rugby. Boys really are great that way. I can't help wondering, if as a group of girls, we would be half so welcoming to a female newcomer.

The day is almost over, and has been 'experience' free. Izzy and I have double drama for our final two periods. Drama is by far my favourite lesson. This is in no small part due to our teacher Mr. Lennox, whose teaching is inspired. The drama rooms and theatre are in a separate building on the opposite side of the school from the main building. No sooner have I started crossing the square, when Izzy catches up with me. She is a little out of breath from running, so I slow down for her. She links her arm through mine. Once her breathing has returned to normal she says,

"Juno, how are you? How are you coping?"

Without looking at her I can sense she is not far from tears. In truth, I feel like having this conversation as much as I feel like sticking rusty pins in my eyes. I try to put myself in her shoes. If it had been Izzy's mother Tina who had passed away, I would definitely feel the need to connect with her. With this in mind I am as honest as I can be.

> "It's really hard, Izzy, and the worst thing is, when it isn't hard, and I find myself feeling alright, just for a moment, the guilt is overwhelming."

> "Oh Juno, she was such an amazing person. Her family was all that mattered to her. I am sure those moments, when you find yourself feeling normal, are the ones she would want you to have more of, not feeling guilty for."

Izzy is such a genuine person, but she doesn't know the whole story. I'm sure if she did, she would feel very differently. The tears come now, for both of us. Izzy digs out some tissues before putting her arm around me. By the time we have crossed the school, we have both pulled ourselves together.

There are only a handful of students in the drama theatre when we arrive. Mr. Lennox comes towards me, holding out his hands for mine. I am terrified, but try to keep it from showing on my face; there seems no way out at this point without seeming terribly rude. I brace myself, as he takes my hands, and am ready...

I am sitting in a spacious nondescript office, facing a man in a white coat sitting behind a huge desk. There is a woman in the seat next to me. We are holding hands. I assume this is Mrs. Lennox. The man behind the desk is unsmiling, leaning forward as he speaks, looking directly at the woman next to me.

> "Unfortunately, the test results confirm that the tumour is malignant."

The hand holding Mr. Lennox's is now gripping it instead. As he turns to meet her eyes, I am left in no doubt that the tumour is hers…

I am back in the drama class. Mr. Lennox has let go of my hands, and is looking at me worriedly. Once again, I go through the motions of satisfying the people around me that I am fine, when clearly, I am far from it. Mr. Lennox tells me how terribly sorry he is about what happened to my mother. Tears are welling in my eyes. While some of these are definitely for my mother, some of them are for him as well.

Toby is the last to arrive; it must be confusing trying to find your way around a totally new place. Izzy takes care of the introductions. Mr. Lennox welcomes Toby to our drama group. He tells the rest of the class to get on with their work, taking Toby and I aside. He explains that last lesson everyone began working in pairs to produce a short piece of work, which will account for five percent of our total grade. The final pieces will include eight still frames. They will be punctuated by darkness. When watched in sequence, the eight frames will depict two people, either moving from harmony into conflict, or progressing from conflict to a resolution. Each performance will last no more than four minutes. As Toby and I are the only two not already in a pair, he suggests we work together. We will spend the next few lessons planning and rehearsing. The finished pieces need to be ready to be performed for the rest of the class this time next week.

Toby and I move to a corner of the room to begin. We quickly decide to do a piece on resolution, and start brainstorming ideas. I dig out my drama journal and start making notes. Toby is easy to work with. He comes up with lots of ideas, also listening attentively to mine. Before long, we have settled on the basic details of the first seven frames. Toby suggests that in the final frame, we should be facing each other, palms touching. It is hard to explain why I don't want our palms to touch without sounding like a total basket case. So

I agree, hoping that by the time this happens, I will have worked out how to stop this madness.

Sophie and I ride the bus home mainly in silence. This is so unusual, but for the life of me I can't remember what we used to talk about. Rather than being strained, the silence is comfortable. She is my oldest and closest friend. Sometimes words aren't necessary. I put my head on her shoulder. We sit this way until we reach Sophie's stop. She squeezes my hand before getting up, and off the bus.

As the bus pulls away, I watch her retreating form, noticing her slumped shoulders, her heavy walk, so different from her normal gait. It helps to remind me, I am not the only one hurting.

Everything has changed, but at times it is as though nothing has. I am sitting in my room doing homework, just like I would have before. I am lost in a world of trigonometry. When a key sounds in the front door lock, I am brought back to the present with a thud. I used to be able to tell by the sound of footsteps in the hall, which of my parents had come home first. Never again will I hear the sound of my mother's heels on the floorboards.

Six-thirty comes and goes with no call from Rosie. The clouds of dementia have descended again. I can only hope they won't claim her for long.

# Chapter 15

I am in a hammock swaying gently. A knotted rope presses into my back. The sun shines on my face while a gentle breeze blows against my skin. Above me is a canopy of tall trees, beyond them a clear, blue sky. I am not alone. Someone is next to me. Our bodies fit perfectly together, side by side. I do not need to look to know it is Mum. She is humming a soothing melody. I feel the urge to look at her face. I move towards her. She is so close but I can't quite see her. I turn a little. I am still unable to catch sight of her. I twist even more. No matter how far I angle my head, I can't find her. My body is contorted. I begin to feel frantic. I start calling for her. I rotate further still. Suddenly I am falling. Waking with a start, I lie still, heart racing. Recalling a relaxation technique Mum taught me when I was younger, and used to suffer from night terrors, I visualise my body filling with a bright, white light starting at the crown of my head and ending at my toes. It takes about five minutes but when I am done, my breathing has normalised.

Lying here feeling guilty isn't helping Dad. Pushing the thoughts aside, I get up, shower, dress and head to the kitchen to make breakfast.

Dad has had the same idea. He is in a suit, pulling the toaster out of its home below the stovetop, on which a frying pan is already warming. He has clearly decided to go back to work today. This is probably a good sign. Somehow it feels like a betrayal. One more thing that will go back to the way it was, before the world as we knew it ended.

I get eggs from the fridge, while Dad goes to the bread bin. Together we prepare breakfast in companionable silence. The radio is on in the background. We don't discuss the fact that Rosie didn't call last night. We both know what it means. Her remarkably long spate of good days had to come to an end sometime. I almost envy her the blissfully ignorant state she is now in.

My stone stomach seems set to stay. Dad's appetite isn't great either, so my food shuffling goes unnoticed. I make a few attempts at conversation. Dad replies to my questions but his answers are short, succinct. He seems tired and preoccupied. Instead of trying in vain to recreate the colourful breakfast exchanges we used to have, I leave him to his thoughts.

Our bus rides to school used to be so full of talk. There never seemed to be enough time to say it all. Everything has changed. Conversation has all but dried up. Sophie is a big believer in dreams. For something to say, I tell her about the dream I had on waking. Sophie is convinced that paying attention to dreams can help to determine what is currently on our minds, reveal our needs and uncover our deepest desires. She even believes they have the power to help discover what the future might hold.

After her grandmother passed away, Sophie became convinced she was communicating with her through her dreams. She believed her grandmother was trying to guide her, to warn her about times ahead. She has several books on dream interpretation and maintains her own dream journal. With great difficulty, I manage to describe my dream to her without crying. Her pleasure at being able to help me is patently obvious. I understand how difficult it has been for her to watch me suffer. All the while powerless to do anything.

Sophie and I have chemistry. I dread seeing Mrs. Eaton. I haven't seen her since Mum's accident. Now I also know things about her I have no business knowing. Seeing our approach through the open door, she immediately walks towards me, arms open. Her face expresses a mixture of sadness and pity, eyes brimming with tears. I have no option. I go to her. As her arms envelop me…

I find myself sitting at a beautifully set table, metres away from the sea. Sun glints on the water. Several boats bob about. Brian Eaton is sitting opposite, talking earnestly at me.

> "Kerrie, words aren't enough to tell you how sorry I am for the hurt I have caused. Lily's death was so sudden and tragic; it crystallised things for me. You need to know that you are the love of my life. You, Jamie and Giselle are all that matter to me. I vow to spend the rest of my days proving to you that giving our marriage another chance was the best decision you ever made. I want us to renew our vows."

With this, he produces a small blue velvet box. He opens it, before sliding it across the table, revealing a solitaire sapphire ring. A hand that is not mine moves to a neck that is not mine. A voice that is not mine exclaims, "Oh Brian, it's beautiful!"…

I am back in the classroom. Mrs. Eaton gently releases me. My relief and happiness for her are so strong; it must show on my face. She looks at me curiously. I quickly alter my expression to a more appropriate one. Still holding my hands she says, "If you need any help with anything at all, please don't hesitate to come to me."

As I sit by Sophie, it dawns on me – that scene was a happy one. For the first time, the memory was not a horrible one. Just knowing that the potential to see positive events exists makes me feel instantly lighter. It still seems incredibly wrong, being privy to the intimate details of people's lives. I am struck by the thought that Georgie would be revelling in my situation. The Gift would be like a dream come true for her.

Mrs. Eaton is a good teacher, managing to make chemistry relatively enjoyable. The time passes quickly. Once the bell goes, Sophie and I part ways. As I make my way to my physics class, Ollie walks up to me, slinging his arm around my shoulders. I automatically stiffen, preparing for the inevitable, only to find nothing happens. Ollie doesn't seem to have noticed. As the tension slowly drains from my body, he chats away amiably. I am so amazed that I am still firmly planted in the here and now, I have no idea what he is talking about.

I spend most of my physics lesson, trying to understand why touching Ollie has no effect on me. Several times I deliberately touch him again to be absolutely certain. I get the same result each time. By the end of the class, the only explanation I can come up with is that it has something to do with Ollie himself. Either that, or I am suddenly cured of the Gift.

My final period for the day is maths. Toby finds me outside the classroom, opening the door for me. I send him a smile of thanks. He tells me he has been thinking about our drama piece; he has some ideas he wants to run by me. They are excellent. I can see it coming together well. Still, I feel some trepidation at the thought of our palms touching in the final scene. We have double drama first thing tomorrow, so I don't have to wait long to get it over with. I lose myself in trigonometry, which isn't hard to do.

There are times during the school day when I can put what has happened to the back of my mind. Once home, as soon as I close the front door behind me, it becomes increasingly difficult. Here, the fissure left by my Mum's death is startlingly present. A yawning void that must be carefully negotiated lest you make one misstep and fall into its unchartered depths.

I spend my time doing schoolwork until Dad comes home. Dinner tonight is lasagna, courtesy of Georgie's mum. I have no idea how long this generosity will continue, or what will happen when it ends. For now, I am grateful that neither of us has to deal with shopping, preparing, or cooking food. It is enough of an effort just heating it, eating it, and clearing away after.

Neither of us comment when 6:30 comes and goes. It is not unusual for Rosie's bad days to come in pairs, or even run for three and four days straight. When the phone rings at 6:40, we look hopefully at one another. Dad answers the phone, his disappointment almost immediately evident on his face. It is Sophie. Dad passes the receiver to me. Sophie has been busy interpreting my dream of this morning.

According to Sophie, my dream reveals that I have plenty on my mind. This is laughable, but knowing how seriously Sophie takes it all, I stay quiet. She tells me my dream means that what I need right now is an escape from reality, responsibilities and problems. I can't find anything to argue with there. Sophie then explains that dreaming about a hammock means my deepest wish is for psychological, moral and spiritual support. She interrupts her flow, reassuring me that she pledges to be there for me, to provide me with all the support I need. She sounds so earnest, so ardent; I am on the verge of tears. Would she still feel that way if she knew the truth about Lily's accident? Lastly, in relation to the future, Sophie assures me the hammock symbolises the serenity I will encounter, after the stormy period I am currently enduring. I thank her profusely, telling her she has given me a huge amount to think about, before saying goodbye.

Before falling asleep, I return again to the puzzling question of Ollie. I come to the conclusion that it is due to his particular psychological makeup. He is the most emotionally steadfast person I know. I have known him for years, and can honestly not remember seeing him upset, worried or nervous, *ever*. Even when he was stretchered off during last year's rugby final, sporting both a dislocated shoulder and concussion, he still wore a smile. We were full of anxiety and concern for his well-being. He was as calm as ever. I am still mulling this over when finally I drift away.

# Chapter 16

I am walking on a bridge of planks, over a deep ravine. The handrails are knotted ropes. I have to tread carefully, as the gap between planks is very wide. The bridge is a long way from the ground. Looking ahead, I can't see where it ends. There is not a soul in sight. I keep progressing slowly forward, not sure why I am here, or where I am going. I am no longer alone. I sense my mother close by. She is right behind me. She speaks softly to me, telling me to keep going. I can feel her breath on my neck, as she gently urges me on. She is so close I can smell her perfume. Instinctively I know that if I turn around, I won't be able to see her. If I turn around, this will end. So I keep looking resolutely ahead, enjoying the comforting sound of her voice, and the feeling of tranquillity that flows from just being in her presence. She tells me she loves me. I start to reply, to tell her that I love her too, that I am so sorry for what I did… I am jerked awake by the sound of my alarm.

Breakfast is another quiet affair. Mum was the one who played the music and kept up a steady stream of chat, entertaining us with tales about her customers at Juno's. It was never forced or strained. Now the silence is deafening. Even the background music we occasionally remember to turn on isn't capable of penetrating the vacuum. The three of us together made something beautiful. Dad and I are like two ends of a necklace. Our clasp is missing. We are still connected, but somehow damaged, fractured, unable to be the whole piece of jewellery we once were.

Perhaps time will change this. Maybe we will find a different way of connecting. Creating something altogether new, something wonderful in its own way. For now, it is like we are living side by side, like flat-mates, with little in common other than our place of abode. Communication is the key. Of this, I am certain. Fear stops me from opening up. Once I start, how will I stop? Then, he will know my secret. He will know that his soulmate is gone forever because of me.

Instead, I make small talk. I tell him I have been in touch with the surgery, letting them know to expect me back at work this Saturday. He is surprised. I reassure him that keeping busy is the best thing for me right now. What I don't say is that when I am at home, the heaviness is inescapable. The atmosphere is viscous. Instead of nitrogen and oxygen, the air here is made of grief and guilt. Is it because everything here reminds me of Mum? Or is it because being here with Dad means I am constantly reminded of the suffering I have caused?

It is only my fourth day back at school. Already, judging only by the way people are treating me, it would be possible to forget what has happened. Momentarily bumping into people no longer affects me. As Izzy and I arrive at the drama theatre, I see Mr. Lennox. I am reminded of his wife's illness. Looking at him, you would never guess that he is experiencing anything distressing in his personal life. It helps to know that I am far from the only person going through a difficult time. Sophie always tells us that if we want anything, we only need to ask the angels. Right now, I send them a quick request for Mrs. Lennox's full recovery, just on the off chance they are listening.

Mr. Lennox starts the class with a short film. Almost ten minutes later, when the film has finished, Toby is yet to arrive. Although I am hugely relieved I won't have to touch him, I am also disappointed. Something about him makes me feel lighter when he is near. Possibly it is because having never known Lily, he is incapable of stirring any memories of her.

Just as Mr. Lennox is assigning me the job of directing another pair, Toby bursts through the doors. He is apologising, grinning at the same time. My happiness at seeing him outweighs my anxiety at touching him. As he makes his way towards me, a genuine smile forms on my face.

We sit in the corner of the theatre to discuss our piece. Very quickly, we finalise the eight frames we will work with. Having resigned myself to the fact that I will have to touch him, I just want to get it over with. We move to the stage area to pace it out. This way, we know how many steps need to be taken between each frame, to end up facing each other, centre-stage, for the final frame.

In the first frame, we will stand on either side of the stage, facing away from each other, feet apart, with our arms folded and heads bowed. When the lights go on for the second frame, Toby will not have moved, but I will have taken a step towards him. I will now be facing him, arms wide, mouth open, as though pleading. In the third, he will remain unmoved, and I will be another step closer. I will have turned my back on him again, and will stand with my arms by my side, shoulders slumped and head bowed, looking utterly resigned. In the fourth, I will stay that way, but he will be closer. He will have turned to face my back, and will have both arms extended, palms open, imploring me wordlessly.

As we move through the scenes, I become increasingly uneasy. Finally, we are face-to-face, arms bent like goal posts, palms facing each other. Our hands touch…

I am instantly standing in a darkened room, looking out through a slightly open door into a dimly lit hallway…

Without warning, I am back in the drama theatre, standing centre-stage, my arms bent, palms facing outwards. Toby is a few paces away. He is looking at me, more curious than worried, perhaps a little nervous too. I smile, to show him all is well, just as the bell rings. Ollie was the exception then. The Gift is still with me.

This is the first time I have seen so little of a memory. I have no idea what it was about. Strangely, rather than feeling relief at not seeing something dreadful, I am genuinely interested to know what happens next. I feel guilty that I am spying, but I can't deny my curiosity is piqued.

It suddenly dawns on me that as soon as I am no longer touching someone, my vision ends. Every other vision I have had has been when someone was hugging me, or touching me for an extended period of time, like when Nurse Rachel took my pulse, or when I had my head in Izzy's lap. This is the first time that the contact has been so brief. Maybe, if I can touch Toby for a bit longer, I might be able to see the entire memory. Then again, perhaps I only get one chance. After all, nothing happened when I touched Dad or Izzy a second time. It's possible, that when I touch him again, I will see nothing, rather than the complete scene. There's only one way to find out.

We have one more session tomorrow before our final performance. We also have double maths today, right before lunch. If I can find a way to touch him, I might know more. The irony of this situation is not lost on me. I have spent the last ten days, desperately trying to avoid touching anyone. Now, I am planning to go out of my way to touch Toby.

I spend break trying to come up with a plan. By the time the bell goes, I have one. As Sophie and I head to biology, she asks me if I have had any more dreams. I don't feel ready to talk about this morning's dream. I lie, telling her that if I have, I don't remember them. Something in the way she looks at me suggests she doesn't believe me. Being Sophie, she doesn't push. We are continuing with the topic of genetics. It is relatively easy and extremely interesting, so the time passes quickly.

In order for my plan to work, I need to arrive in class after Toby, so I hang back a bit in the lab. Toby is already seated when I walk in and I take the empty seat next to him. Opening my pencil case, I place my pen near my left elbow, between the two of us. Turning to the right, I bend down to take my maths workbook out of my bag on the floor - and as I sit up, I deliberately knock my pen to the floor. Both Toby and I turn, bending to retrieve it. Our hands meet...

I am back in the dark room, staring through a partially open door. I see a figure in a pink bathrobe at the other end of a hallway...

As quickly as it came, the vision is gone. Does the fact that I was seeing almost exactly the same memory as before confirm my suspicion that I am yet to see the part that created an emotional response in him? My mind is a whir. I realise I am looking at the floor, my arm still outstretched to collect my pen that is no longer there.

I am not sure exactly how long I have been like this. It can't have been too long. I straighten up, turning to face forward. Toby is holding my pen, looking at me askance. This is hardly surprising. I smile as normally as I can, thank him, take back my pen, and start copying down formulae off the board. The teacher announces we will have a trigonometry test tomorrow. I make a concerted effort to put Toby's memory to a corner of my mind, focusing my attention on the lesson.

Walking to the playing field for lunch, Toby seems more reserved than usual - probably a result of my odd behaviour. I need to explain myself somehow. I feel certain that I have still not seen Toby's entire memory. How can what I have seen be responsible for creating any strong emotion in him? Things are only going to get stranger, at least until I have seen his memory fully. I don't really know what to say. I don't have much time before we are with the others so, rather than over-thinking it, I just talk.

"I want to explain about before." At this he nods encouragingly. "I suppose you know that when I heard about Mum's accident I passed out?" Again he nods, urging me to continue.

"I imagine you've also been told that I was unconscious in hospital for a couple of days?"

"Yes, Georgie explained everything. I hope that's ok."

"Of course! Well, anyway, ever since then, I keep getting these dizzy moments. It's like I zone out. I'm not actually unconscious, but it's almost as though I'm not there. It's pretty strange, but the doctor says it's nothing to worry about."

"Wow - that must be really weird. Scary too I'd imagine."

Little does he know *how* scary.

"To be honest, I think it's far scarier for the people around me. It actually feels a little like I'm asleep."

And having horrible nightmares, I think to myself. Toby looks somewhat relieved. I am pleased to have that out of the way. It will make tomorrow's drama rehearsal much easier.

Dad and I are still in the kitchen clearing up after dinner when the phone rings. It is after seven; we both know it won't be Rosie. He makes a move towards it but I stop him with a gesture. For the first time since I came home from the hospital, I answer the phone.

"Hello? Juno speaking."

"Just the person I was looking for," says a voice, unmistakably Toby's. I feel my face heating up. I am so thankful he can't see me; Dad can though. He is looking at me, clearly wondering who has elicited this reaction.

"Oh, hi..." I stammer stupidly. Smiling weakly at Dad by way of explanation, I take the handset out of the kitchen, heading towards my bedroom.

"Is everything ok?"

"Yes, of course, sorry, I was just busy with something." I am so flustered, it is hard not to babble incoherently.

"Do you want me to call back?"

"No, no, it's fine. I can finish later."

"Well, I won't keep you, I was just wondering if you wanted to come and see a movie with me on Saturday?"

"Oh... Uh, sure, I'd love to..." I manage to mutter. Suddenly, remembering my intention to return to work I add, "But it will have to be after three. Is that ok?"

"That's perfect. Have you seen *Date Night*? It's still showing and is supposed to be hilarious."

"No, I haven't seen it."

"Great! Well, I'll let you get back to what you were doing. See you tomorrow."

"See you."

My heart is beating fast enough for me to feel it. My cheeks are still burning. What is going on? Less than two weeks ago my mother was killed because, thanks to me, she was somewhere she wasn't supposed to be. Here I am feeling happy. What sort of a person does that make me?

I take the phone back to the kitchen, pretending not to notice how curious Dad is. Mum would have asked me outright but that isn't Dad's style. I kiss him goodnight, telling him I have a maths test tomorrow that I need to revise for.

# Chapter 17

I am woken by the alarm. If I have been dreaming, I don't recall anything. Somehow, not dreaming at all is worse than the haunting dreams. Two weeks ago today, my mother was alive. Lying in bed, I try to remember our last breakfast together: what we ate, what songs played in the background, what Mum was wearing. She had been excited about our dinner out that evening, but that's all I am able to recall. If only I had known how much those details would mean to me now. If only I had paid more attention. Instead, I was caught up in trivial plans for a meaningless party.

The mood at breakfast is even more melancholy than usual. Dad has made a decision that cooking huge breakfasts neither of us actually eats is a waste. Today, we have fruit salad. We talk little about nothing of consequence, eating even less. Although we are living through exactly the same nightmare, we are doing it separately.

Out of the blue, he explains that Mr. Fitzgerald, our headmaster, contacted him, offering the services of a grief and loss counsellor.

Without meeting my eye, he says he has spoken to her. If we decide to go ahead, she would like to meet each of us singly first, before seeing us together. Shock renders me speechless. I seriously can't think of anything I would rather do less than talk to a total stranger about the wreck that is my life. To buy myself some time, I ask if I can think it over before giving him an answer. Once that is off his chest, he seems less burdened.

As Sophie boards the bus, she looks at me expectantly. I am not sure what she's waiting for. Ignoring her, I start to rant about counselling sessions I don't want to have. In true Sophie-style she patiently hears me out, before gently suggesting that maybe Dad feels the counselling might be beneficial for him.

"Perhaps you will be doing him a big favour by going along with it."

It takes Sophie's suggestion to make me look at this from Dad's point of view. My selfishness knows no bounds.

"Don't forget, Juno, counsellors are properly trained to deal with situations like yours. Seeing one couldn't possibly hurt. You might even find a session or two quite helpful yourself."

When she puts it like this, it is hard to argue with. The thought still turns my stomach.

"Is there anything else you want to tell me?"

She is smiling suggestively. It takes a few moments before I realise what she is alluding to.

"So that's how he got my phone number!"

She is grinning widely now. I can't help but smile back at her.

It's not until break that I see Toby. He is sitting on the field talking to Ollie, his face in profile as Sophie and I approach. For the first time, I allow myself a proper look at him. His face is long, with a high forehead. He has a head of thick, brown hair, cut short at the back and sides. His nose is straight, his cheek bones prominent. He really is a good-looking boy. They notice us approaching. He smiles broadly up at us.

It is hard to understand how one brief phone conversation can have changed things so dramatically. All of a sudden, I am ridiculously nervous. My instinct is to sit as far away from him as possible but I resist this temptation as I know it could be easily misinterpreted. Ollie is totally oblivious, rambling on about some rugby match, which takes the pressure off me having to make conversation. Soon everyone has arrived. The boys break off as usual to play something involving a ball.

Maths is right after break. I am tempted to sit apart from Toby so as not to be distracted, but he catches up with me so I can hardly sit somewhere else now. The test is hard, but I think I have done enough to pass. I am certain that even if I haven't, I will be allowed to re-sit it, so I don't allow myself to worry too much. I can tell that Toby didn't struggle at all, but he is sensitive enough to tell me it was a difficult test.

The boys have a rugby training session at lunch, so it is just the four of us for the first time in what seems like forever. It is a beautiful autumn day. We lie side by side on the edge of the field, listening to music Georgie plays on her phone. I am not ready to share the news about my movie date with Toby just yet. True to form, Sophie seems to intuit this without being told.

Toby arrives in the drama theatre before I do. Mr. Lennox has given us the whole double period to finalise details of our performance pieces, including costumes, lighting and timing. Each group is assigned a five-minute slot on the stage and ours is towards the end. We begin by discussing exactly how many seconds we will hold each frame for, and how many seconds of darkness there will be in between them. Toby initially suggests that we hold each frame for ten seconds, with fifteen seconds of darkness. I am fairly certain that the longer our palms touch in the final scene, the greater chance I'll have of seeing his whole memory. Instead, I propose that we hold the frames for fifteen seconds each, with ten seconds of darkness in between. He happily agrees, and we start discussing our costumes.

We decide to wear white t-shirts over white pants, with buttoned up black overcoats on top. The plan is to shed the overcoats in the darkness between the penultimate and final scenes, so that in the reconciliation scene, we will both be in white. The darkness between the final two scenes will be longer, so we will have enough time to unbutton and remove our coats. In the final frame, instead of two spotlit areas, both spotlights will be trained on one position.

Eventually, it is our turn to use the stage. We move through the frames and Mr. Lennox times us until we are standing face-to-face, palms touching...

I am back where I was before, looking into a darkened hallway. From the other end of the corridor, a fair-haired woman in a pink dressing gown enters the scene. She is dragging something on the floor behind her. As she walks closer, I can see that it is a pillow. The way she walks suggests complete and utter exhaustion. It is almost as if she is sleepwalking. She crosses the hall and enters a door on the opposite side of the hallway...

I am on-stage, facing Toby, our palms still touching. Toby is grinning as Mr. Lennox congratulates us on a great job.

I am relieved, but now have even more questions than before. That wasn't like any of the other visions I have experienced. Nothing really happened. What sort of emotions could that innocuous scene arouse? Who is the woman in the dressing gown? Toby's mother? There must be more to the memory than that. My face must reveal my confusion because Toby says hesitantly,

"It seemed to go well don't you think?"

"Yes, I think it went very well, and Mr. Lennox seemed to really like it too."

The bell goes signalling the beginning of the weekend. We say goodbye to Mr. Lennox, and I wonder what his weekend has in store for him and his wife.

Toby, Izzy and I make our way out of the theatre back towards the main building. Izzy is unhappy about her performance partner Jackson, who she thinks is lazy and disinterested. She is already looking ahead to the next group piece, when the three of us can work together. She goes off to meet Jasper, telling Toby she will see him at rugby tomorrow, and signalling that she will call me.

Ollie captains the 16A rugby team. Izzy and her family watch every game. Personally, I don't know how she does it. I go to the inter-school final each year, only because it is compulsory, but spend most of the game with my hands covering my face, peering through my fingers, while boys, some as big as men, throw themselves at each other and at an unyielding turf. My job at the surgery means that where my friends are concerned, I have a legitimate excuse to miss these weekly torture sessions. Toby explains that he will play half a match for the Bs, and a half for the As, following which the coaches will decide where he best fits in. I wish him luck. We agree to meet outside the cinema at 5:15 tomorrow for a 5:30 showing.

Sophie is waiting for me at the bus stop. Normally, our weekends are filled with sleepovers, get-togethers, shopping outings and parties. Hardly a weekend went by when we didn't spend at least one night together, but I need to take things slowly. I can't imagine leaving Dad alone in the house all night just yet and the thought of anyone else spending the night with us is an equally uncomfortable one. I know Sophie will wait until I am ready, and that no explanations are necessary. As she gets off the bus, I promise to call her after the movie.

We sit down to a tuna pasta bake for dinner, smiling knowingly at one another. Mum hated tuna with a passion, believing it was only good for cats and not fit for human consumption. It is a bittersweet moment for us both.

I tell him a little about my day, including the drama performance. Mum would have known all about it, and would be helping me sort out my costume. Dad never gets involved in the minutiae of my days the way she did. Tonight, he is making a big effort to take everything in, to be both Mum and Dad. He listens intently as I tell him about the new boy at school and all about the drama piece we have to perform together. He asks lots of questions, and I do my best to answer them.

Then I broach the subject of the movie tomorrow. It feels so awkward talking to him about this kind of thing. Ordinarily I would have this sort of chat with Mum, in my room, definitely not in Dad's presence. I have never given much thought to whether or not she discussed these things with Dad later, as it never mattered. I work to keep my voice neutral, eyes trained on my fork as I use it to move the food around on my plate rather than meeting his eye. If I were having this conversation with Mum, she would have a million questions for me, but this information seems to stop Dad in his tracks. He seems genuinely pleased that I have plans, but is happy to leave it at that. I can see how incredibly hard this is for him. I just wish I knew how to make things easier.

Now seems to be the perfect time to tell him I am prepared to go to the grief counsellor.

"I just wanted to let you know that I've had time to think about it, and have decided that going to see the grief counsellor is a good idea."

The positive effect this news has on his mood is remarkable. Despite feeling ill at the thought of what lies ahead, I am glad of my decision.

A call from Rosie would be wonderful, but as the hands of the clock slide past 6:30, I slowly lose hope. Dad and I watch an old black-and-white movie on television. Mum loved old movies, and she would have really enjoyed this one. The space she used to fill sits solidly between us. If only we could find a way to reach across the crevasse for one another. For now we have to be content to occupy opposite sides of it.

# Chapter 18

A wall of mirrors surrounds me. I turn around slowly, eyeing the myriad versions of myself as I do. Just as I am about to come full circle, my reflection begins to alter slowly. The changes happen so subtly, they are difficult to pinpoint. Before long, I am not recognisable. I stare intently at the face opposite me. Eventually I realise, I am now looking at Mum. She looks directly into my eyes, smiling peacefully. I reach out to touch her. She does not mirror my action. Instead of her warm, soft skin, my fingertips find only the cold, hard surface of glass. I move a little closer to the mirror. Her image starts to fade slightly, as though I am looking through a fine vapour. I move closer still, watching as the mist thickens, causing her image to dissolve even more. I get as close as I can, pressing my face to the glass, trying to reach her. The fog is so thick now, her face has disappeared from view altogether. Now there is nothing in front of me at all.

My heart is racing. It takes a while for the frustration I felt in the dream to pass. Once I am calmer, I get up and go to the kitchen for something to eat. Glancing at the calendar, I notice it is the first of

May. We are no longer in the month that Mum died. My mum died last month. This knowledge hits me hard, obliterating what little appetite I had. Leaving the kitchen, I get ready for work, preoccupied with the thought that with every passing moment, we move interminably away from the time when she was with us.

Just as I am about to leave, Mrs. Young arrives. I haven't seen her since the accident. Her face crumples at the sight of me. Before I have a chance to say anything, she has her arms around me, her face buried in my neck…

I am immediately transported into a cluttered sitting room. I am sitting on a large, coral-coloured, velvet chair with lace covers on its wide arms. A phone starts ringing. It takes me some time to get out of the chair and over to the phone that is sitting on a counter, dividing the room I am in from a galley kitchen.

"Hello," says Mrs. Young in her quavery voice.

"Ivy?"

It's Rosie's voice, one that I have been longing to hear, but not like this.

"Mrs. Dixon, is that you?"

"Yes, Ivy… it's me. I'm so sorry, but I have some… awful news."

She is audibly crying, a sound I have never heard before and never want to hear again. It is heartbreaking.

"What is it, Mrs. Dixon? Please tell me? Is it Juno?"

"No Ivy… it's not Juno… It's Lily. There was an accident… She's been…killed."

Rosie's sobs are more than I can bear…

It is a huge reprieve to find myself holding a sobbing Mrs. Young in my arms. Unsurprisingly, I too am in tears. Dad comes to see what's going on. Mrs. Young lets go of me and now clings to Dad, who is fighting back tears. He gestures over her head for me to leave. I can't deny feeling relief at the respite I have been offered, as I close the door behind me.

In hindsight, I am pleased I refused Dad's offer of a ride to work. The walk to the bus stop gives me time to calm down. I don't have to wait long for the bus to arrive and thankfully I have a seat to myself the whole way. Thinking ahead about how many people I might potentially have to touch today, I am beginning to question my decision to return to work so soon.

The sight of the dry cleaners sends shockwaves through me. This is where Mum was headed that fateful Friday. I had totally forgotten that I would have to pass it today. My legs start shaking. It feels like I am wearing a corset that is way too tight and I can't breathe. I have less than fifty metres to walk to the surgery. It may as well be fifty miles. Nausea threatens, so I stop, leaning my back against a chemist's front window. Closing my eyes, I sit down and hang my head between my knees, hoping to increase the blood-flow to my brain. After a while I check my watch. I have only minutes till I am due to start work so I stand up and somehow propel myself forward. The surgery is on the fifth floor of a large office tower but fortunately I am alone in the elevator the whole way.

I have to walk through the waiting room to enter the surgery. Only one woman is there, sitting reading a magazine. There used to be two doctors in the practice but Dr. Richmond is the only one there now after his partner retired. He has two nurses, Lucy and Sue, who work on rotation. Saturdays are generally quite busy, but we still manage to find time to talk. During the time I have worked with them, I have found them both extremely friendly, and easy to be with.

Sue is in her late twenties, a petite, pretty, brunette. She is not married but enjoys a very active social life, often describing her weekend activities to me in detail. Lucy is a little older than Sue, married with two sons. Physically, she is Sue's opposite, tall and broad-shouldered with closely cropped, blonde hair.

A passing glance into the nurse's room reveals Sue, who is on duty today, weighing a lanky teenage girl. Hearing me pass, she turns to look at me. Her smile is warm, yet simultaneously expresses deep sadness. I acknowledge her with a small smile. I continue past Dr. Richmond's door, which is closed, meaning he is either with a patient or on the phone.

My job mainly consists of answering phones, making appointments, taking payments, chasing pathology results and handing out referrals or scripts left for collection. I also cover for the nurse on duty when she has her lunch break. As surgery is generally busier on Saturdays, Dr. Richmond works through lunch. The nurse's break only lasts half an hour, but during this time I have to weigh and take the blood pressure readings of patients, before they go in to see the doctor. The scales are the old-fashioned type, where you have to move weights along a bar to get an accurate reading. The blood-pressure machine is old-style too. Dr. Richmond spent several hours with me when I first started teaching me how to read the results. Anything more complicated than that has to wait until after the lunch break.

Once Sue has accompanied the girl back to the waiting room, she walks into the open-plan area that houses the reception desk.

"Juno, I just wanted to tell you how awfully sorry I am. What a terrible tragedy, you poor thing. How are you coping?"

Here's an interesting thing I have learnt recently; once I cry on any given day, the chance of me crying at some point later that same day is markedly increased. This morning's episode with Mrs. Young means that tears will never be far away today. They are here now, pooling in my eyes. In order to stop them in their tracks, it is imperative that I avoid speaking right now.

Sue sees the struggle I am having. In an attempt to relieve me of the need to speak, she leans over to give my shoulder a squeeze...

At once I am in a brightly lit hospital corridor, with a group of people I have never seen before...

I am pulled back to the present. Sue is looking at me nervously. She has pulled back her hand, as though touching me has spooked her, rather than the other way around. I reassure her that I am fine. She doesn't seem totally convinced but smiles weakly at me before retreating to her room.

A sliding, one-way window, built into the wall above my desk, allows me to look directly into the waiting room. The lanky teenager is now sitting with the lady I passed earlier. I watch as an elderly man arrives. Glancing at the appointment book, I note that all but two of today's appointment slots are booked. The phone rings. As I am taking details from an elderly woman, Dr. Richmond emerges from his office with a patient. I have known this man all my life. He knew Mum for all of hers. His look conveys it all. The sympathy in his face is too much for me to endure. I am thankful for the patient here with us and the one on the end of the line, otherwise I would no doubt be in pieces. I avert my gaze, getting on with the job at hand.

The morning passes quickly. It is not until Sue asks if I'm all right to cover for her that I realise the time. Looking into the waiting room, I notice only one person in there. A small, pretty woman sits absolutely still. She seems to be staring at a spot on the floor in the centre of the room. When I follow her gaze, there is nothing there. Perhaps she is daydreaming. I wonder if this is what I look like when I am having one of my visions. There is nothing scary about her, but who knows what memory I will tap into? Swallowing my nerves, I assure Sue that I will be fine but I sense her genuine concern. Although I appreciate it, I am acutely aware that the sooner she starts her break, the sooner she finishes it, thus the fewer patients I will have to deal with.

Taking her records with me, I walk to the waiting room door and ask the patient to come with me. She is a petite, dark-haired woman, with eyes so brown they are almost black. I ask her to step onto the scales sensing her hesitation. Being weighed does that to most women, so I think little of it. She removes her shoes, stepping on the scales. I write her weight on the card, noting that it is several kilograms below the one recorded on her last visit, a matter of weeks ago.

I am careful to sit down before fitting the cuff of the blood pressure apparatus to her arm. I inflate the cuff, mentally preparing myself before placing my fingers on her wrist to monitor her pulse...

I am on my back, lying on a hard, narrow bed, with my top raised and pants lowered, so they sit on my hips. My stomach is fully exposed. Next to me stands a woman in a pale blue cap and gown, with her back to me. Opposite me is a machine resembling an outmoded television displaying incomprehensible white blurs on a black background. The woman is moving a cold probe over the skin of my belly. The probe is moved, stilled, pressed into me more strongly, and then repositioned.

This sequence is repeated a few times. All the while, the uniformed woman stares at the screen.

"Is everything alright?"

Although I haven't heard her voice, I know it is my patient speaking. When the other woman doesn't reply immediately she continues.

"Please tell me… is everything ok with my baby?"

The uniformed woman turns around, sadness etched into her face. She replies softly but clinically,

> "I'm very sorry Mrs. Wade, but there is no longer a heartbeat. Given the size of the foetus I would guess that it died a few days ago."…

Mrs. Wade is sitting opposite me as if in a trance - her gaze now fixed at a point on the wall behind me. Looking at the machine, I realise I have missed seeing the reading. I apologise for the delay, which barely seems to register. I begin the whole process again. Looking at her, it is as though an impenetrable bubble of sadness surrounds her. Perhaps this is how I appear to people at the moment. I gently guide her back to the waiting room until Dr. Richmond is ready for her.

In the interim, a middle-aged man has arrived and is now seated. I hope with all my might that Sue will be back before I have to deal with him. As if in answer to my thought, both lines begin ringing at the same time so for the next little while, I am tied up on the phone. Finished with his current patient, Dr. Richmond retrieves Mrs. Wade from the waiting area. As I am helping the outgoing patient to settle his account, Sue returns.

As three o'clock approaches, I am exhausted. Thinking about what will happen if Dr. Richmond wants to hug me or hold my hands is frightening. He must bear witness to more horrifying things than most. More worrying, however, is how on earth I will explain my turn to *him*. My standard, 'the doctor said it's nothing to worry about' line, won't wash here. In order to avoid a scene, I tell Sue I am in a hurry to be somewhere else. She readily agrees that I can leave a little early so I make my escape while Dr. Richmond is occupied with his last patient. As I exit the building, I turn right rather than left, so as not to pass the dry cleaners again. It means a slightly longer walk to the bus, but a bit of exercise is preferable to seeing that place again.

Mrs. Young is gone by the time I get home. I find Dad reading on the couch. Mum used to collect me from the surgery every Saturday on her way home from Juno's. Once home, we would ritually have a cup of tea together before I went to meet the girls for whatever our weekend festivities included. Dad offers to make tea now. He has been grocery shopping and has bought my favourite biscuits. Together we drink tea and dunk biscuits. The conversation doesn't exactly flow, but the quiet spaces in between are comfortable.

I gladly accept his offer to drop me at the cinema, which pleases him more than I would have ever imagined. I have been working so hard to convince him that I am coping and that he needn't worry about me. Oddly, he is never happier than when he is doing something for me. As we pull up outside the cinema complex, Toby is there waiting for me. I point him out to Dad before kissing him goodbye. As I hop out of the car, I remind him to send Rosie my love in case she calls.

Toby already has two tickets and refuses my offer to pay for one. Now this really feels like a date. The nerves I have managed to stifle all afternoon start to surface. As we walk into the cinema, he takes my hand. Momentarily, I stiffen and experience a flash of panic, but this is an altogether different feeling. I am right here, where I should be. My heart is racing wildly. My body temperature begins to climb steadily. He smiles down at me. I try not to look like a mouse about to be devoured by a tiger. It's not as though I've never held hands with a boy before. Yet somehow, this feels totally different. We choose seats in the centre of the theatre and Toby goes off to buy snacks. I do my best to use the time to calm myself down.

The movie is ridiculous but so funny that for the first time since before Mum's accident, I am laughing loudly, totally in the moment. Toby takes my hand again as we leave. I cope marginally better this time. We are both still smiling as we reach the street. It is dark, but still early, so we decide to go for pizza. We talk about the movie, reliving the funniest scenes, laughing all over again. I feel happy, relaxed. Hot on the heels of this is my close companion guilt. I feel so good that for now, I push the feeling aside. There's plenty of time for that later. Toby is so easy to talk to, even easier to listen to. He has an endless repertoire of interesting and entertaining stories.

It is only 8:30 but Toby insists on taking me home. It is out of his way, but free-flowing conversation is something I have sorely missed lately, so I don't put up much of a fight. Toby is talking about a new movie due out next month. My attention is diverted when something about a girl across the road catches my eye. She is tall with red hair almost down to her waist. Although we are on opposite sides of the street, I realise with a shock that I am looking at Piper Reid. She is wearing a short denim skirt, very high heels, and a tight, black, strapless top. I am stunned by the gaping difference between the womanly figure I see tonight, and the demure schoolgirl with the extra long uniform I sit next to in history. I am still staring awkwardly, as she walks into the crowded Sheaf Hotel. I drag my attention back to Toby and what he is saying.

Although it is early, I don't invite Toby in. I am not ready for him to meet Dad just yet. I sense no disappointment. As we say goodbye, he leans towards me, gently placing a kiss on my lips. Once he reaches the footpath, he turns, smiles and gives me a wave, which I return. I watch as he walks away before closing the door behind me. I lean on the closed door, heart racing, weak-kneed. Once I have composed myself, I walk into the living room. Dad is curled up, asleep on the sofa, in front of the television. The guilt I had so thoughtlessly pushed away not long ago returns with a vengeance I am ill-prepared for. I get a blanket from the hall cupboard, laying it over him before turning off the television.

Taking the telephone into my bedroom, I dial Sophie's mobile. She answers after the first ring. Speech fails me, but tears do not. Sophie says nothing, allowing me to cry until after some time, my sobs peter out. I tell her how good I was feeling less than an hour ago. I explain how horribly guilty I feel about experiencing happiness at a time like this. What I don't tell her is that my guilt is compounded, because I am the one responsible for my mother's death.

Sophie asks me if I have given any thought to the timing of Toby's arrival. I am way too tired and emotional to understand where she is headed with this line of questioning. I tell her as much, trying in vain to keep the frustration out of my voice. None of this is her fault, after all. Sophie patiently explains her theory: that Lily sent Toby to me to help me deal with her passing. Not for the first time, I find myself wishing I could see the world through Sophie's eyes.

# Chapter 19

We leave for Greenfields around 9:30. The sky is overcast, threatening rain. Dad tells me Rosie didn't call last night, so we need to be prepared for the worst. To lighten the mood, I tell him about last night's movie. Before long, we are both laughing at the scenes I recount. It is a great sound and an even better feeling.

About twenty minutes into the drive, Dad tells me he has arranged for a real estate agent to sell Juno's. A scorching wave of anger surges up inside me. Tears threaten, prickling my eyes, while my throat constricts. Resolved not to cry, I say nothing. Instead, I stare fixedly out the window. Outside her family, Juno's was the most important thing in Mum's life yet only two weeks after her death, Dad is planning to sell it.

As suddenly as it came, the anger is gone, leaving only a scalding shame in its wake. What right do I have to be angry? If it weren't for my self-indulgence, none of this would be happening. Who did I imagine was going to run the shop without Mum here to do it? I have been so self-absorbed. Not once have I considered the fate of Juno's. Dad has had to make this decision, along with many others, alone, with no support from me or anyone else. Not trusting my voice, I reach out my hand, placing it on his arm, hoping to communicate understanding. He smiles sadly. It is abundantly clear that this decision makes him just as unhappy as it does me.

As we approach the reception area, my thoughts turn to Rosie. As far as I can remember, five consecutive bad days are the most she has ever had. If today is another bad day, it will be her sixth in a row. She isn't in the reception area, but given the weather, that's not surprising. We make our way to the lounge. When we can't find her there, we look on the balcony. The only other place to check is her room. Chances are, if she's there, it's another bad day. There are two kinds of bad days. There are those when she has no idea who we are. Despite this, she is happy to see us, confusing us for people that were part of her life seventy years ago. On these days she is animated and friendly. The other kind is much worse. Sadly, today is one of the latter.

Rosie sits in an armchair. Her head is bowed so far forward that her chin rests on her chest. You could be forgiven for thinking she is asleep. We know better. On these days, she is filled with an intense paranoia. Experience has taught us she has deliberately lowered her head at the sound of our approaching footsteps. She is scrunching her eyes shut so tightly that her whole face contracts much as a young child pretending to be asleep might. Every so often, she squints her eyes open, keeping her head lowered throughout, peeking, her eyes darting from side to side, searching for evidence of someone in the room. As soon as she senses that someone is near, she squeezes her eyes shut again, tucking her chin further into her chest.

The first time we saw Rosie like this was enormously distressing. Soon after, Mum and Dad scheduled a meeting with the medical team to discuss her condition. The staff explained that regardless of how Rosie is on any given day, our visits are absolutely vital. Her deterioration has been much slower than anticipated. She has exceeded their expectations on all indicators. The doctors are convinced the constant contact with family and the regularity of our visits are the things keeping Rosie well. Their advice, for days like this one, is to continue as normal, attempting to engage her wherever possible; not losing hope when it isn't.

Taking her to the lounge when she is like this is out of the question. Despite Rosie's obvious discomfort at our presence, we sit on chairs facing her, informing her about our week. Like a relay team, we take turns talking. When one runs out of steam, the other picks up the baton, continuing the one-sided conversation. Mum was far more proficient at this than either of us. Despite our best efforts, eventually there is nothing more to be said. The three of us sit in morose silence. On days like these, we don't stay for lunch. When Rosie is this bad, she has to be fed. It is a difficult ordeal, even to watch.

Something about this place is soporific. Within an hour or so of spending a Sunday visit indoors, I am continually stifling yawns, fighting to keep my eyes open. Not for the first time I wonder if there is an air-borne sedative being pumped through the air-conditioning system here, to keep the residents more manageable.

The drive home after a visit on one of Rosie's bad days is never an easy one. Today is no exception. We are both talked out. The radio provides a welcome distraction. Rosie's illness will eventually progress to the point that her good days will disappear altogether, but I refuse to believe we have reached that stage. If Sophie is right, if Mum really is somewhere wonderful using her influence to make good things happen for us, Rosie will have stretches of good days for a long time to come.

# Chapter 20

I wake from a dreamless sleep, well before my alarm is due to go off. Lying in bed, I try to conjure up the image of my mother's face in my mind's eye. I fail miserably. The harder I try, the more difficult it becomes. The idea that one day I won't be able to imagine her face at all fills me with dread. I get up, go to the lounge, and pull a few photo albums down from the shelf. Mum was the photographer in the family. As such, there are loads of photos of me on my own, of Dad alone, and plenty of the two of us together. There are far fewer with Mum in them. Sadly, given Dad and my photographic skills, many of the ones she does appear in are out of focus.

I flip through a few albums, finally finding a picture of the three of us taken at Teya and Eliot's first birthday party. I slip it out of the plastic pocket, bring it back to my bedroom and place it on my bedside table. I want it to be the first thing I see each morning. Mum is wearing an aqua blue halter-neck dress. Her hair is swept up and back in a French knot. Her face is framed on either side by big, but delicate, gold-hoop earrings. Although there are three people in the picture, something about the way the light is hitting Mum means she is the one your eyes are drawn to. She looks directly at the camera. Her smile, so warm and generous, comes as much from her eyes as it does her mouth. Her face is so lovely. Looking at her actually hurts.

While we are waiting for the kettle to boil, I notice Dad has been marking Rosie's bad days on the calendar, just like Mum used to. When Rosie was admitted to Greenfields, the doctors explained that keeping a record of her different types of days was one way of discovering if there was any kind of pattern in the way they occur. They also explained that it might help them to pinpoint the time when Rosie begins losing her battle against the illness, which might give them a chance to make changes to her treatment before it becomes too late. The staff at Greenfields records everything. Regardless, Mum always did too. She argued that nobody knew Rosie as well as we did. If any patterns were going to be uncovered, they would be more likely to be done so by us.

If Rosie isn't good today, there will be seven consecutive marks on the calendar. This is the most there have ever been. Dad and I pointedly avoid talking about this. Instead, I talk about my drama piece tomorrow, briefly describing the requirements and outlining the frames we will perform. He asks a few questions, which I answer. The conversation we aren't having heavily overshadows the one we have.

Seeing Sophie as she gets on the bus lifts my spirits. She is the one person I have always felt comfortable discussing Rosie with. In part, this is because she has known Rosie all her life. The subject of Rosie's illness was almost taboo with Mum and Dad so whenever I have been particularly concerned about it, Sophie is the one I have turned to. We rarely talked about it at home because we were all scared to admit it was actually happening. Without Mum here, nothing has changed. Rosie's good days are so good that they make it possible to imagine that the bad days aren't important. A run of difficult days like this one makes denying her illness impossible.

Sophie is quiet throughout. Only after I have finished airing my darkest fears does she speak. She suggests that Rosie may have received the news about Lily's accident and my hospitalisation at the same time. This is most likely the case, and something I had not considered. Sophie points out that Rosie might have somehow managed to stave off her illness to stay strong for Dad until I had recovered and for both of us during the funeral, as well as for a considerable stretch of time beyond that. Sophie believes that once Rosie saw we were both relatively alright, she allowed her own grieving process to begin. This actually makes sense. More importantly, it gives me a far more palatable explanation for what is going on with Rosie because what Sophie doesn't know is that on top of everything else, Rosie has also had to deal with the arrival of the Gift into my life. I can always count on Sophie not only to hear me out, but also to give me an alternative, more appealing way of looking at things. Laying my head on her shoulder, I tell her how lucky I am to have her in my life.

After first period biology, I have maths. Toby is waiting for me in the hallway outside the classroom. There is something incredibly comforting about the sight of him standing there, looking out for me. I walk towards him, and we enter the classroom together. Our test results are back. I am relieved to find I have passed, although my fifty-eight percent is a little less impressive next to Toby's result.

We walk hand in hand to the playing fields. I watch as Georgie and Izzy's faces register this development. Clearly Sophie has said nothing to either of them. For this, I am grateful although it now means I have some explaining to do. Georgie is desperate to know everything, but Toby's presence means she has to wait. Her eyes are literally popping out of her head with the effort required to keep quiet. The second the boys are up playing football, Georgie and Izzy are on my case, demanding information. I do what I can to satiate their desire for details. Once the inquisition is over, they are genuinely happy for me.

"He's a brilliant rugby player, Juno. All the coaches were impressed on Saturday. He will definitely be in the A team on a regular basis," reports Izzy. I try to look suitably impressed, but in truth, the whole rugby thing leaves me cold.

It isn't until Piper sits next to me in history that I remember having seen her on Saturday night. The contrast between this prim schoolgirl and the glamorous, leggy creature I saw just days ago is even more startling in the light of day. It seems I am not the only person keeping one aspect of her life a secret. Perhaps we have more in common than I thought.

There is a message from Dad on the answering machine when I get home, explaining that he will be late. It gives me an opportunity to go through Mum's cupboard without having to upset him. Our final drama performance is tomorrow and I need to use Mum's black overcoat. I walk into my parents' bedroom for the first time since the accident. Mum's absence is even more noticeable in here than it is in the rest of the house. I wonder how my poor father is coping, sleeping in an otherwise empty bed with her things all around him.

I open her wardrobe. The sight of all her clothes that will never be worn by her again knocks the wind out of me. It feels like someone has thrown a huge cement ball into my stomach. My knees give way. I slide to the floor, dissolving into tears. I do nothing to stem the tide. My body jerks as huge heaving sobs erupt. Weeping like this, it is hard to imagine I will ever be able to stop.

It takes time. Eventually, the intensity subsides and I am reduced to keening like a banshee. At some point, I fall silent. I lay where I am until the hitching in my breath passes and I can stand up. I wipe my face and move back to the open wardrobe, where I take out her overcoat. I bring it to my face, deeply inhaling her scent. It is a mixture of her favourite perfume and a fragrance that was uniquely hers. The aroma is embedded into the fibres of the coat's lining, much as it is in my memory.

Over a dinner of beef stroganoff, Dad explains the reason he was late. He had his first session with the counsellor. Her name is Sylvia. He found her to be compassionate, empathetic and very easy to talk to. Maybe I am imagining it, but he does seem slightly more at ease tonight. If talking things through with a complete stranger is going to help him get through this, I am all for it.

"I have made a tentative appointment for you to see her tomorrow after school. Let me know if that's not good for you as I can easily change it."

I try to keep the horror I feel from showing on my face by pretending I am working on an extra chewy piece of beef. I swallow before replying,

"Tomorrow afternoon is fine," in a voice that doesn't sound nearly as self-assured as I'd hoped.

Six thirty comes and goes, marking a full week without a call from Rosie. I am in my room working through my trigonometry test when, a little after eight, the phone rings. Dad brings it to me announcing that it is Toby, a hint of a smile playing on his lips. I pull a face as I take the receiver from him and close the door. A call from Rosie would have been wonderful but this alternative comes pretty close. We chat a little about school, before he gets to the reason for his call.

"I'm just letting you know that I won't get to school until after lunch tomorrow. I wanted to warn you, in case you were worried about me missing the drama performance. I promise I will definitely be there in time for that." He doesn't tell me where he is going, and I don't ask.

Despite having had an 'experience' free day, I am shattered. I read a few chapters of *Great Expectations* before going to sleep.

# Chapter 21

The sun is shining brightly. I have to shield my eyes from its glare. I am somewhere up high. Looking down, I can see streets far below me. Miniature cars drive around while even tinier people walk on footpaths. I am on a ledge, hundreds of metres above the ground. I hear Mum call my name. She is right in front of me, wearing her blue halter-neck dress. Despite the height, she walks as confidently as if we were on the ground. I call out to her, begging her to be careful. She turns, smiling at me, reaching out her hand towards me. As I reach for her, she slips off the ledge. I shriek as she begins to float downwards. She descends in slow motion her hair and dress billowing around her. She still wears that wondrous smile. Just before she reaches the ground, in an all too familiar gesture, she blows me a kiss.

I am flat on my back, staring at the ceiling, heart hammering in my chest, sweat breaking out all over my body. I begin to cry, curling into a ball on my side, hugging my pillow to my face to stifle the noise I am making. When at last I remove the pillow and open my eyes, her beautiful face is staring back at me.

Sitting in maths without Toby next to me is a strange feeling. Stranger still, since I have only known him a matter of weeks. Our teacher seems to have been pre-warned about his absence. What could be so important that it has to be done on a weekday during school? Time seems to drag. It takes a determined effort to stay on task.

Thoughts of my up-coming counselling session plague me all day. I realise I need to go through with it for Dad. I also understand that unless Sylvia is a magician, there is nothing she can do to make things better for me. I resolve to divulge as little as possible, without being overtly rude. I just need to get it over with as swiftly and painlessly as I can.

Izzy and I arrive at the drama theatre after Toby. He smiles at us as we enter; however, he seems slightly subdued. Perhaps he is a little nervous about our performance. Most of us have been at school together at least since year seven. This will be his first time to perform in front of any of us. Mr. Lennox asks us all to get into our costumes, ready to perform. Izzy and I go to the dressing rooms to change.

When we return, Toby is already seated in one of the front rows. There are no empty seats near him, so Izzy and I find spaces where we can. When the whole class is ready, Mr. Lennox passes out a list showing the order in which we will perform. Toby and I are listed third, two places ahead of Izzy and Jackson. It is too warm to wear the coat now, so I keep it on my lap. I enjoy the first two performances, which are both very different. When they are finished, Toby and I stand, each walking to opposite sides of the stage. I put on the overcoat and am enveloped in my mother's scent. It fills me with sadness, yet at the same time it manages to make me feel like she is right here with me. The lights go down. I get into position.

We move smoothly through each frame. As the lights go down after the seventh, I quickly remove Mum's coat, moving to stand with my arms bent at shoulder height, palms facing out. Toby's palms touch mine...

I am standing in what looks like a hospital room. There is a woman in a wheelchair with her back to me. A large man is standing next to me. I watch as he walks forward, taking hold of the handles of the wheelchair before turning it round to face me. The woman, who I can see clearly now, has fair hair hanging limply around her puffy face. Her skin is extremely pale. Her features are expressionless. Her head is inclined slightly to the left, mouth agape. Her eyes are open, staring vacantly ahead, seeing nothing at all.

"Sharon, look who's here to see you," the gentleman standing opposite me says...

The class is clapping. Toby looks at me inquisitively. He obviously noticed that I zoned out briefly. To cover for me he stood with his palms against mine until I checked back in. I smile gratefully at him as we move apart, going back to our places to watch the remaining performances.

I notice little about Izzy's or anybody else's pieces as I am consumed by my thoughts. What is going on? I just saw another memory of Toby's! This is the first time I have had two entirely different experiences with the same person. I was happily deluded into believing that once I had a complete experience with someone, that was it. I assumed I could move that person into the safe category, meaning the Gift was no longer a problem where they were concerned. I was obviously mistaken. This is the Gift that keeps on giving. The implications are ghastly. Why didn't I see this vision when we held hands yesterday? Is it possible this memory has something to do with his absence today?

After class, we all make our way back to the main building. I am apprehensive about touching Toby again. As though he is able to hear my thoughts, he makes no move to take my hand. Notwithstanding my relief, I can't help worrying why he doesn't. I try not to read too much into it. I am comforted when, as we part ways, he tells me he will call tonight. I have more pressing things to worry about - my counselling session this afternoon being one.

I arrive fifteen minutes early. The receptionist gives me a form to complete while I wait. As I finish filling in my details, the door to Sylvia's office opens. A woman around the same age as Mum walks out. I can tell she has been crying. I pretend to re-check the details on my form until she has settled her account. Minutes after she has gone, the door re-opens. I am summoned in.

I'm not sure exactly what I expected Sylvia to look like. This is not it. She is about five foot tall, not counting her hair, which is blue-black, cut short at the sides and gelled into long spikes on the top of her head. She has caramel-coloured skin, and is solidly built. She is dressed in tight black jeans, a body-hugging fluorescent orange top and a black denim jacket. Silver-studded, black ankle boots complete the look. She smiles warmly at me, the skin around her eyes forming huge creases as she welcomes me, and indicates my seating options. There is a small sofa, two armchairs and a single straight-backed chair, all placed around a low coffee table, bare but for a large box of tissues. Bookshelves line walls on either side of the room, the back wall is predominantly occupied by a large window.

I choose to sit on the sofa, while Sylvia sits on the armchair to my right. She starts by telling me how sorry she is to hear about my mum's passing. I accept her condolences, intent on saying as little as possible. She then asks me how I am coping. There is something about her, something so far removed from my idea of a counsellor that begins to melt my steely resolve. Despite my determination not to, I begin to cry.

I find myself opening up to her in a way I hadn't foreseen. Initially I speak haltingly, explaining how difficult it has been for Dad, trying to be both mother and father to me. I tell her I have tried to make things easier for him. I want him to know I am fine and that he doesn't need to worry about me. Once I start talking, I can't stop. The floodgates are open, and everything comes pouring out. I tell her about how things were before. The three of us were so great together, the closest of families. Mum was the talkative, exciting, entertaining one. In contrast, Dad and I are both quieter, generally happy to stay in the background. Mum was the one who shone, the one people were drawn to. She was the one who lit up the room. Mum played the leading role. That was the way we liked it. Now that the main attraction is gone, all we have left is the supporting cast.

She tells me she has only two questions for me.

"Firstly, do you love your father?" My answer is an immediate, definitive yes.

"Secondly, you are only sixteen, correct?" I nod by way of an answer.

"So, why is it that you feel responsible for your father's happiness?"

This question does me in. Before I know it, I am bent over double, wailing into my lap. She makes no move to comfort me, except to move the tissues closer. She waits patiently until my howling has abated to mere sniffles, and I am again able to speak.

"Because it's my fault that she's dead!"

There, I have finally said it out loud, although it is really more of a whisper. It actually feels good to get it off my chest. I look at Sylvia, expecting a look of contempt but instead see something wholly unanticipated - pure and unadulterated compassion. There is not the slightest hint of distaste or judgement. Encouraged, I go on. Between shuddering sobs, I tell her about the call I made to Lily that morning, asking her to collect my dress from the dry cleaners. I explain that it was all because I selfishly wanted to go shopping with a girlfriend. This is the reason Mum was in the car at that hour. This is why she was not safely behind the counter at Juno's, where she should have been.

Like a river whose banks have burst, there is no way of arresting the flow; the tears persist in a steady stream. My face is buried in my hands...

Before I know what has happened, I am standing on the kerb at a busy intersection. Clearly, Sylvia is touching me. I am at the front of a group of people, waiting for the lights to signal it's safe to cross. I am surrounded by people. I am holding a mobile phone, reading an email displayed on the screen.

"Cory," comes a woman's voice from behind me. Her tone is one of frustration, annoyance even.

"Cory! Cory!" The woman is shouting now, an edge of panic has crept into her voice. Someone small knocks into me. I look down as a boy of about three, clutching a plush panda bear, brushes past me, running headlong into the traffic. Sylvia's instinct to protect the child is defeated by her own instinct to survive as a massive, silver, four-wheel drive bears down on him. I watch helplessly as the vehicle slams into the boy, sending his tiny body flying upwards in a perfect arc before gravity takes over, hurling him forcefully onto the asphalt. The car's brakes are screeching horribly. People are screaming. The smell of burning rubber fills the air. A woman pushes roughly past me, collapsing to her knees beside the boy. The sound that emits from her seems barely human. It is heart-wrenching. She begins to wail one word over and over.

"No, no, no, no." A pool of blood has formed underneath the boy, visible only because the woman now cradles his lifeless form in her arms. The last thing I see is the panda, lying face down metres away from the little boy, as the one word mantra continues…

Thankfully, the scene is over. I am once again staring at my lap. The brutality of that memory has halted my tears. Sylvia sits next to me, speaking to me, her tone soothing. I can't make out the words over the sound of my heart drumming in my ears. I keep my face lowered until I have managed to calm myself, which takes a while. When I look up, she is smiling at me. I attempt to listen to what she is saying.

"You can think about it between now and next session." I am clueless as to what I am supposed to be thinking about, but I nod as though I am in full agreement. Sylvia stands up. I realise she means for me to stand too. Putting her arm around my shoulders, she gently guides me to the door, signalling the end of our time together. Dad has taken care of the account, so in less than a minute, I find myself back on the street. I wonder when the scene I just saw actually took place. It makes little difference now. There is no question in my mind that poor little Cory is gone - just like Lily.

Dad is eager to know how things went with Sylvia. I am still stunned I revealed as much as I did. I don't understand what came over me. I can't take it back now but I'm not sure I would, even if I could. The stone in my stomach feels marginally smaller. I actually find myself eating a little more dinner. I tell him I found her friendly, warm and easy to talk to, just like he did. I can see how pleased this makes him. He reminds me that we are due to have a joint session and agree that he will arrange it for sometime next week.

Our spirits lift even further when the phone rings at 6:30. We both move to answer it, and then simultaneously stop to let the other one get it, before both moving for the phone again. We are both laughing as

Dad grabs the phone, handing it straight to me. It is Rosie. The relief in the room is palpable. Just the sound of her voice makes everything seem better. She sounds weary, but otherwise fine. Inevitably, after a run of bad days, her first good day is a difficult and often tiring one. Given how many bad days she is coming off, she will no doubt be exhausted today. According to the staff at Greenfields, she often becomes irritable. We never see this side of her. With us, she is always loving and patient.

It is an unspoken rule that we don't discuss Rosie's bad days with her. I am not about to change that. I tell her a bit about what's going on at school and that I have started back at the surgery. I ask after Eric, who is recovering well. Not wanting to tire her even more, I pass the phone to Dad.

I am expecting Toby's call, so have the handset in my room when it rings. We chat a little about the drama performance. I sense there is something else he wants to talk about and I do my best to give him the opportunity to speak. Either he doesn't know how to raise the topic or it's my imagination. The conversation is definitely more stilted than normal. This only serves to make me more nervous which in turn makes it harder for me to talk. Not surprisingly, the conversation doesn't last long. I am left feeling disappointed although about what I'm not entirely sure. I watch some television with Dad before going to bed. The upside of days like today is that I am too exhausted not to sleep.

# Chapter 22

Sophie is eager to know how the session with Sylvia went. Telling her about it, without revealing the reason for Mum's accident, or anything about my Gift, is near impossible. I hate hiding secrets from her. She is so open, honest and trusting. I have never kept a secret from her before. I don't believe she has ever kept one from me. Now, I am keeping two. It's hard not to feel like I am betraying her. Regardless, I don't feel ready to tell her about my visions. It's not that she wouldn't believe me. She is far more likely to believe me than almost anyone I know. Maybe it's because I don't fully understand them myself yet; I am reluctant to open up to anyone other than Rosie.

Despite having confessed to Sylvia, I still don't feel ready to tell anyone else about my part in Mum's accident. Sylvia is a professional being paid to listen to me, to help me. She never knew Lily. No matter what she really feels about me, about what I did, her job requires that she remain neutral, at least outwardly.

So, without going into details, I tell Sophie it was very positive, and in an attempt to make up for what I'm not saying, I mention seeing Piper on Saturday night. I describe her outfit down to the last detail, and tell her where I saw her going. Once I am done, Sophie is as perplexed as I am.

"Do you know who her friends are?" she asks. "I mean have you ever seen her hanging out with anyone else at school?"

When I think about it, Sophie is right. I honestly can't recall ever seeing Piper talk to another student. I don't remember her spending time with any group at break or lunch. The more I think about her, the more of an enigma she becomes.

"Perhaps she's on a covert mission!" laughs Sophie. We spend the rest of the bus ride creating outlandish fantasies about Piper Reid, international spy. It is juvenile beyond words. It feels incredibly good to be laughing together, the way we used to.

As I am walking to the field for break, Toby catches up with me. It is the first time I have seen him today. I am eager to see whether things seem normal between us or not. He doesn't try to take my hand. As I am far too shy to initiate anything, we walk side by side. Everyone is at the field when we arrive so there is no opportunity for us to talk properly. He definitely appears much more relaxed than yesterday. He sits near me, smiles at me, directs conversation towards me, and is as friendly as ever. Still, I can't help worrying that things have changed.

Once the bell goes, I am up and making my way to class. I am lost in thought, continuing to wonder if Toby has decided he doesn't like me that way any more. My train of thought is interrupted when he asks if I am free this Saturday night. I am taken aback, not quite sure I heard him right. Registering my confusion, he repeats his request.

"Absolutely!" I answer, relieved he still likes me, and pleased to have something I can genuinely look forward to.

Piper is already seated next to someone when I walk into history. I sit at the desk directly behind her. We are spending a double period learning about the Treaty of Versailles. Mr. Hardy is not particularly inspiring, regularly veering off on irrelevant tangents. Today is no exception. I am certain that one or two people in the class ask specific questions in a deliberate attempt to steer him off track. They are almost always successful.

I am absent-mindedly gazing at the back of Piper's swanlike neck when I notice something on her skin, just where the top of her shirt collar sits. I've never noticed it before, but I guess I have hardly paid a huge amount of attention to Piper at all until recently. It is black, and looks like a line drawing of two arcs next to each other just like the scrawl a child would use in a drawing, to show a bird flying. It can only be a tattoo, but what does it represent? The more I learn about this girl, the less I realise I know, the more of a mystery she becomes.

I don't feel like sharing this discovery with Sophie. To begin with, I might be mistaken; perhaps it isn't a tattoo at all. Also, I have started to feel bad that we joked about her earlier today. I realise that, for some odd reason, I have begun to feel a little protective of Piper. Instead, I talk to Sophie about Toby.

"Yesterday he seemed withdrawn and distant. He was like a different person. It may have been nothing to do with me, but I noticed it when he called last night. It was the most difficult conversation we have had. It felt as though he had something to say but couldn't or didn't know how to."

"How did he seem today?"

"Better, almost the same as before, but things still feel different." I'm embarrassed to mention he hasn't held my hand since Monday for fear of sounding obsessive.

"He asked me to spend Saturday night with him. Do you think he wants to tell me that he just wants to be friends?" This is a stupid question. No matter what she actually thinks, Sophie would never say anything to intentionally upset me.

"Of course not!" She answers emphatically. "What could have happened since Saturday night to change his mind?"

As always, Sophie knows exactly what to say, to make me feel better, although my fears are not totally allayed. Tomorrow, I have both double drama and double maths, which means I will be with Toby, for half of my eight lessons. By the end of the day, I should have a pretty good idea where I stand.

I always look forward to my conversations with Rosie. Tonight, I am almost desperate. I am careful to let Dad answer the call as I plan to speak to her from the privacy of my room. I am in the kitchen, not intentionally listening to Dad's half of his conversation, when he interrupts Rosie to tell her he will put her on speaker so I can hear what she has to say.

"Oh, Aaron, you are ever so clever. Juno, darling, are you there? Can you hear me?" In stark contrast to last night, her voice sounds strong, full of life.

"Yes, Rosie, we're both here." Dad winks at me. Rosie is constantly amazed by today's technology, generally acting as though we are complete geniuses for just knowing how to apply it.

"Right, well, as I was saying, I had a lovely visit from Astrid today. We have written to each other quite regularly since she left. Her sister, the one she went to take care of, the one with the cancer in her liver, well, she passed away about two months ago."

There is an awkward pause. I don't look at Dad, instead keeping my eyes trained on my lap. I can't help wondering how long it will be before the mention of somebody losing their life won't have this effect on us. Perhaps that time will never come.

"Anyway," Rosie continues, her voice a little shaky now. "Astrid stayed in her sister's home, helping her niece sort through things. The house is now on the market, and Astrid doesn't have many friends in Brisbane, so she decided to move back to Sydney."

Rosie is definitely working up to something but I haven't quite worked out what yet. "She has found a small apartment, it's on the train line, and well, I was thinking… Since the two of you are so busy with work and school, and don't have time for cooking and cleaning, and since Astrid has no job at the moment, it might work out well for everybody if she came and helped you out."

It's hard to argue with this logic. Astrid is a known quantity, somebody we both like. More importantly, she is somebody we trust. Given the fact that neither Dad or I have any talent where cooking is concerned, and the neighbourly generosity we have been shown to date can't go on endlessly, Rosie's solution seems perfect. Looking at me, shrugging his shoulders, Dad says, "Well, it sounds like you've solved everybody's problems in one fell swoop!"

He takes down Astrid's mobile number, promising Rosie he will call her tomorrow, before turning off the speaker. Once they have finished talking, Dad gives me the handset. I chat generally about my day for a while until Dad moves to the lounge to read. He seems not to take any notice of me as I walk past him and towards my bedroom.

Once inside, I fill Rosie in on the experiences I have had since we last spoke properly. I start with Mr. Lennox, telling her I witnessed the delivery of his wife's brain tumour diagnosis. I recall the reconciliation scene between Kerrie Eaton and her husband. I recount the devastating ultrasound result that Mrs. Wade received, before relating the traumatic death of the little boy Cory. Next, I tell her that Mrs. Young was here on Saturday. I describe the phone call she herself made to deliver the news of Mum's accident. I don't believe she had any doubts about the veracity of my visions before. If she did, my detailed recounting of her conversation with Ivy Young puts them to rest.

Then, I move on to the two most interesting developments. I begin by explaining how Ollie touched me, causing no effect at all. I wait before going on, giving Rosie time to absorb this. She knows who Ollie is, although she doesn't know him well. I run through my theory for her. Rosie agrees that Ollie's even emotional temperament may be the answer. Before revealing the most puzzling thing, I briefly fill her in about Toby's arrival at school, and our pairing up for the drama recital. I go on to detail the first vision that touching him produced. Like me, she is confused about what the scene could mean. She promises to give it some thought. Lastly, I reveal the fact that in the final drama performance, when our hands touched, I had a totally different experience. I report the specifics of the second vision to her. Rosie's interest is really piqued now.

"Do you think the women in the two scenes are the same person?" I have been pondering this very same question. I am unaware that I have come to a conclusion until I hear myself answer.

"Yes, I do. Even though I didn't get to see the woman's face in the first scene, I'm almost certain it was her I saw in the wheelchair. They both had fair hair, but that's not it. The thing that makes me believe they must be the same person isn't anything about the way they look. The main similarity between them is the total absence of any energy around them. Does that make sense?"

"Absolutely! Oh Juno! This is all so interesting, my head is spinning. I can't imagine how you must be coping with it all?"

"To be honest, it's so overwhelming, most of the time I don't know what to feel. I thought I had worked out what was happening - that I was seeing people's most recent emotionally charged memory. When I saw those two totally different, almost emotionless memories of Toby's, it totally threw me. Now I feel like I'm back at square one. If only I understood what was happening, I'm sure it would be much easier to deal with."

I hear muffled talking. I realise Rosie is being asked to get off the phone. Sometimes, the Greenfields staff treat their elderly patients like children. It makes me angry on their behalf. Rosie is not one to make trouble, she apologises before we sign off in our usual way.

Just talking through those experiences has been like reliving them, all in the space of half an hour. I am too tired to contemplate anything other than zoning out in front of the television. I join Dad on the couch. Together we watch *Poh's Kitchen*, one of Mum's favourite shows. In this episode, Poh is staying at the home of this week's guest cook in Western Australia's Margaret River. We watch as they catch freshwater marron before cooking it on a verandah, a beautiful vineyard as a backdrop. Watching requires no thought. It is entertaining enough to take my mind off things for a while.

# Chapter 23

"Do you want the good news or the bad?" This has always been one of my Dad's favourite questions. Once I swallow my mouthful of muesli I answer, "I'll have some good news please."

Rolling his eyes dramatically, he says, "Drumroll please... we have a joint counselling session booked for next Tuesday at four fifteen."

"Poor Sylvia!" I joke, causing us both to laugh.

"What's the bad news?"

"That's it, there isn't anything else. I just wasn't sure whether you would think it was a good or a bad thing, so I hedged my bets."

When I arrive with Izzy at the theatre for drama, Toby is standing outside. He seems sincerely happy to see me, which is comforting. He enters with us and I take this to mean he was waiting for us. When he sits down next to me, I am convinced everything between us is just fine and I have been anxious for nothing. Mr. Lennox announces our performance grades. Toby and I are awarded the second-highest mark in the class. I am thrilled. Spontaneously, I raise my right hand to Toby for a high five. He just smiles, winking at me, leaving my hand hovering in space awkwardly. I lower it into my lap, feeling myself blush deeply. Mr. Lennox is now outlining our next performance task, giving me a perfect excuse to bury my face in my notebook. It seems to take forever before I no longer feel flushed and flustered.

"This time we will work in groups of four." Izzy grabs my hand excitedly, the whole room starts buzzing. "But, instead of choosing the group you will work with, I have chosen the groups for you."

This announcement elicits a loud, collective groan from around the room. Mr. Lennox laughs as he passes out a sheet listing the pre-selected groups. He explains that as actors, we need to be flexible enough to perform with whomever we are cast. Once I have the list in my hand, I scan it quickly for my name, finding it in the third group. I am extremely relieved not to find Toby's name in the same group.

Mr. Lennox continues, "Each group will collaborate in devising and performing a piece of original theatre, based on one of the following issues facing teenagers today: bullying, drug and/or alcohol abuse, eating disorders, violence in the media and suicide. The final pieces will need to be no longer than ten minutes, and you will need to be ready to perform them in a fortnight."

We gather in our groups to begin planning. I am determined not to look at Toby. I deliberately seat myself with my back toward his and Izzy's group. Despite feeling awful, I do my best to contribute something to the group. Becoming the self-elected note-taker means I am helping without having to think too much.

I am so confused right now. The idea of spending break with everyone is too daunting. I tell a white lie about needing to see my English teacher. I am hoping this will work as it is the only class I don't share with any of them. I start walking quickly back to the main building instead of to the field with the others. Rather than be discovered loitering in the halls, I decide to go to biology early. The lab is empty, so there is no need to explain my presence to anybody.

I am determined to forget about Toby. I have enough going on in my life without having to worry about anything extra. Once I have made this decision, I feel much calmer. I am seated when the bell goes. The rest of the class begins to arrive and Sophie sits next to me. Just having her close to me helps to cement my resolve. So much so, by the end of the lesson, I feel ready to face anything, even Toby.

He is already seated when I walk into maths class. I plan to sit next to anybody but him. He is beaming at me as though I am the one person in the world he wants to see. I've heard the term mixed signals before, but this is crazy. One minute he is waiting outside class for me to arrive - the next, he can't even bear to touch me and now here he is, looking fit to burst with excitement at the prospect of sitting next to me for the next eighty minutes. Looking at his smile, those eyes, my resolve crumbles. I sit in the chair next to his. Saturday can't come soon enough for me. At least I will be put out of my misery one way or another.

Once again, I allow Dad to speak with Rosie first, before escaping with the phone into my bedroom. I tell her how grateful I am to have her to talk to. She is the only person I have confided in. Rosie says she has done little more than think about the Gift since we spoke last night.

"The one thing the Gift has had in common for each of you is that it is experienced through touch. Frances, Ruby and Mary all had to touch people in order to read them, as do you."

I hadn't thought about it before, but she is right. Rosie goes on to say she believes my theory about Ollie may be correct but also suggests an alternative one.

"Occasionally, my sister Frances would encounter people she couldn't read. It happened only rarely. Frances would be quite frustrated when it did. Our neighbour Daisy was one of these people. She took enormous delight in upsetting Frances by stealing things from her room only to return them days later without Frances ever knowing they were gone. Perhaps Ollie is just one of those people who cannot be read."

This is a possibility that hadn't occurred to me. Unlike Frances, the more unreadable people out there, the happier I'll be.

Rosie also has a suggestion for why I had a totally different vision when I touched Toby on Tuesday. She believes he experienced a new emotive event sometime after the first time I touched him. However, she is convinced that the two scenes are somehow connected. She thinks perhaps they are two parts of the same emotional memory.

"Unfortunately, unless you get to know more about him, we may never know whether I'm right or wrong."

I'm doing my best on that score. I say nothing, other than to agree with her. Then I ask her something that's been puzzling me.

"Do you think there is some kind of time limit on the emotional memory? I mean, how long after someone has experienced an emotional event do you think I will still be able to see it?"

"That's a good question, Juno. One we may never definitively know the answer to. I would hazard a guess that you will be able to read an event until the next more, or at least equally, emotional one happens to take its place."

Although this is not the answer I was hoping for, it is the one I was expecting. This explains why sometimes when I witness a terrifying scene, the owner of the memory seems totally fine. The actual event may have taken place days, weeks or even months before.

Just when I think the conversation is about to end Rosie says, "There's something else that I really ought to tell you."

"I'm not sure I can handle much more right now, Rosie," I reply, only half in jest.

"Juno, darling, I know how difficult things have been. You are grieving. You're having to adjust to life without Lily. On top of all that you have a new Gift, which would have been challenging to deal with under normal circumstances. These circumstances are anything but normal. I understand that you are coping with most of this totally on your own. Please know that I don't for one minute underestimate the enormity of what's happening to you. I have given this a lot of thought, I really have. Despite all that, I honestly believe this is something you need to know now. I didn't want to mention it sooner, as I was afraid of worrying you. It is important though."

This is sounding ominous. To lighten the mood I say, "Ok, Rosie, let me have it."

"Right, well, there is one more thing that Ruby, Mary and Frances' Gifts had in common."

She pauses here. I am curious now, so I urge her to go on.

"Well, in the beginning after Frances was ill, she could tell people what they had in their pockets or elsewhere on their bodies. After a while, and my memory is a little hazy as to how long that was, the Gift seemed to grow."

"What do you mean by grow exactly?"

"I mean it became stronger. It happened fairly gradually. It developed to the point where she could see not only what people had on them, but also how they had come to get it, even where they got it from."

"And this also happened to Mary and Ruby?"

"Exactly. Ruby's Gift became so sharp that she was able to tell you not only what you had eaten in the last twenty-four hours, but also the individual ingredients that each thing consisted of. She could detect the smallest pinch of nutmeg in a cake even if the person she was touching had consumed only one bite of it."

I am almost afraid to ask, but I do anyway.

"What happened to Mary?"

"Well, Mary could initially place her hands on a pregnant woman's belly and tell her the gender of the child she was carrying at the time. Later, she was able to tell them about future pregnancies. She could predict with accuracy how many children a woman would have, what gender, and in what order. Eventually, she was even correctly predicting unviable pregnancies."

Rosie allows a little time for this to sink in. It is all a little unsettling, and I can hear the fear in my voice as I ask, "What do you think this could mean for me?"

"I've thought about that most of the day, Juno, but I'm afraid I really don't know. Only time will tell, sweetheart. I just wanted to let you know that the Gift might start to progress."

"Oh, there's one more thing," she adds. I am slightly nervous about hearing anything else at this point.

"I really think it's important you discuss everything that's been happening to you with someone else, someone other than me. Having somebody else's perspective on your visions might prove very helpful."

This comes as a blow. I am unsure what to say in reply. I don't have to worry as Rosie isn't expecting me to say anything, ending the call in our usual way.

When I answer the phone around eight, I am surprised to hear Toby's voice. I am sensitive to every nuance, detecting only warmth as he laments the fact we aren't in the same group for drama. He sounds so relaxed, so at ease that his mood spreads to me. Soon, we are prattling on about school. I am surprised, when at the end of the call, I find we have been talking for nearly an hour.

As I lie in bed, my thoughts turn to what Rosie said. The idea that my Gift could get even stronger is unbearable. Just trying to imagine the different ways it might change has my mind reeling. I make a commitment to put this new information out of my head for now. If things start to change, I'll deal with them then. I recall Rosie's advice to confide in another person. She is probably right; perhaps, being the only one I can turn to is also putting undue pressure on her. This is the last thing I want to be responsible for. I can't burden Dad with anything else at the moment, so Sophie is the most logical choice. As soon as an opportunity presents itself, I will tell her everything.

# Chapter 24

I am surrounded by ice - as far as the eye can see, in every direction. Although the air around me is cold, I am not uncomfortable. The area of ice I am standing on is quite thin and as I look down through it, a street comes into view. I lay down to get a closer look. Peering at the scene, I notice it is raining heavily. The road is deserted. A person appears on the street. It is a woman. I watch her run, head down, in the driving rain towards a car. It is Mum. She gets into her car, starts the engine, begins to drive. The torrential downpour lashes her tiny vehicle. The windscreen wipers beat furiously, ineffectively, against the ceaseless deluge. Suddenly, I know what's about to happen. I have to warn her, make her stop. I start calling, yelling, hammering my fists futilely onto the ice. Before my eyes, a wall of fire springs up on the street below. I am unable to see anything beyond the flames.

I lay stock-still until the sweat has dried on my skin and my heartbeat has slowed. I turn to gaze at Mum's photo for a while before getting up. Fridays used to have a certain feel about them. No other day felt as good. They had a feeling of promise, as though almost anything could happen. Then one Friday, something did happen. Now Fridays have a totally different feel. Each one marks another week since the Friday our lives changed forever.

The weather outside is dismal, matching the mood inside. Over tea and toast, Dad and I talk distractedly about the weekend ahead. There is a prolonged silence. Without giving it much thought I ask, "Is it alright if I invite Sophie for a sleepover tonight?" He hesitates, but his answer when delivered sounds heartfelt.

"Of course! It will be lovely to see her."

The word 'again' is left unsaid. The sleepover will be another small step towards normalcy. This ought to feel good. In reality, it feels like I am somehow being unfaithful, but to whom, or what I don't know.

"I managed to get hold of Astrid yesterday. She's very keen to come and help us out. She almost made it sound as though we will be doing her the favour, rather than the other way around," he chuckles as he says this.

"It will be really nice to have her around again."

"I'll let Annie know what's happening. I'm certain she has been responsible for the meals on wheels service we have been treated to."

On the bus I ask Sophie if she is free to sleep over, and see her face light up. It is like watching the sun come out from behind a bank of dark clouds. I failed to comprehend just how much she was missing our weekends together. Her mood lifts markedly, highlighting just how subdued she has been lately. She pulls her mobile phone from her bag to send Annie, her mother, a text. When she is done, she links her arm through mine, leaning her head on my shoulder. It feels good to be the one making Sophie happy for a change, rather than the other way round.

The morning goes quickly. After we have eaten lunch, the boys leave for training. Georgie and Izzy are consumed with an upcoming party. They talk about little else but this no longer upsets me. As it doesn't involve me, I am free to lie here, totally zoning out. I think back to last night's discussion with Rosie. I remind myself just how lucky I am to have her. I recall what she said about Ollie, wondering what percentage of the population might be unreadable.

I will do as she suggested. Tonight, I will tell Sophie everything. It will help to have someone else to talk things through with. A frightening thought enters my mind. Is Rosie urging me to open up to someone else because she senses she is getting sicker? I can't bear to think this might be the case. I push the idea aside and tune in to a debate about the best eye makeup to wear with a purple dress.

It feels almost like old times, as Sophie and I walk up the path to our front door. Dad surprises me, calling out to us as we walk into the hall. He greets Sophie with a hug. He has come home early from work, and is making Sophie's favourite meal, roast chicken, for dinner. He tells us excitedly that he has rented a copy of the latest *Cheech & Chong* movie *Hey Watch This* for us to watch together. *Up in Smoke* is Dad's all time favourite film. Over the years, the four of us watched it together countless times, as well as every other *Cheech & Chong* movie ever made.

Sophie and I offer to help him with dinner. It seems he has everything under control, so we go straight to my room. Sophie immediately walks to the photo by my bed. My room is almost as familiar to her as her own. The photograph of the three of us is the only addition to the room since she was last here. She looks lovingly at the beautiful image of my mother.

"She really was such a special person, Juno."

This pronouncement has me close to tears. I fight them back. Sitting on my bed I gesture for her to join me.

"Sophie, I have something really important to tell you."

"Sure, what is it?"

"This is going to sound totally crazy but please just hear me out." She nods. I have no doubt she will do just that.

"When I woke up in the Intensive Care Unit, Dad came to see me. The first thing he did was hug me. As soon as he did, it was like I was transported out of my body into his and back in time. I saw myself at his desk in his office. It seemed like a dream, but something made me certain it was real. It was so vivid. I was actually there. I have never been to his office before, so I knew I wasn't imagining it. I only realised that's where I was when I saw a photo of Mum and I on the desk. Then the phone rang. It was a policeman, calling to tell him about Mum's accident. All of a sudden, I was back in the ICU, a doctor shining a light into my eyes."

To say Sophie looks animated is an understatement. I look into her gleaming eyes. There is not a shred of visible doubt. I am encouraged to continue.

"The next day, when a nurse took my pulse, it happened again - only this time, I was in her home, on her couch, being hit by her boyfriend."

Sophie looks at me in awe although I am absolutely certain that it is more to do with the violence I described than the fact of the vision itself.

"Almost everybody I have touched since then has caused me to have a vision."

I pause to let this sink in.

"When I touched you in biology class on my first day back at school, I saw you in the park, pushing Eliot and Teya on the swings. It was the day of Eliot's accident. I saw him fall off the swing, just the way you saw it. You were wearing your blue top with the owl on it."

If I didn't have her attention before, I certainly have it now. I continue, recounting many of the memories I have seen. I choose not to tell her about Mr. Lennox's wife or Mrs. Eaton's issues with her husband. I also skip the visions I experienced with Toby. These feel too private, too intimate to share, and besides, they make little sense anyway. Even without these, there is plenty to tell. By the time I am done, Sophie's eyes are as huge as saucers. Her mouth is hanging open.

In true Sophie-style, she says nothing for a while. I can almost hear the cogs of her mind working. When the questions finally come, they include many of the ones I have asked myself. I answer the ones I can, and am honest when I can't. I tell her what Rosie has told me about the other women in my family and their versions of the Gift. For now, I make no mention of how their abilities progressed over time. I am still holding onto the possibility this will not happen to me.

Talking about Rosie prompts me to check the clock. My heart sinks when I see it is 6:40. Did Rosie unburden herself last night because she somehow knew she might not have long before the clouds descended again? This is a horrible thought and I do my best to let it go. We are interrupted when Dad calls us for dinner. The next few hours are a welcome break for both Dad and I, although I can sense Sophie's mind is elsewhere. Dad is more relaxed than I have seen him in ages. I am certain this is true of me too. By the time we go to bed, I can barely keep my eyes open. Sophie, still wired after my revelations, is eager to talk. I stay awake as long as I can, which isn't very long.

# Chapter 25

Sophie is already up and dressed when my alarm wakes me. I wonder how much sleep she actually had. She seems so much more energised today than she has of late. Having her here at breakfast makes everything so much easier too. It isn't as though Dad and I are deliberately behaving differently. It's more that Sophie fills a portion of the space Mum used to occupy, making the void smaller, easier to cope with.

The weather outside is as beautiful today as yesterday was dreary. Dad drives Sophie home. Then he drops me right outside the surgery, before going shopping armed with a list supplied by Astrid. There is one woman in the waiting room when I go in. The door to the nurse's room is open as I pass. I glance in, but see nobody so I am startled when I come face-to-face with Lucy in the corridor.

"Oh, Juno, sweetheart, I'm so terribly sorry."

She pulls me to her, wrapping her arms around me...

I am in a garden full of people. We are all facing a suited man, standing on a porch. He is speaking in a continuous monologue, with barely any inflexion in his voice, much like a race caller. As he speaks, he gestures to the house behind him. It is an auction. The man next to me is holding my hand. He clutches it fiercely, before raising his free hand. The auctioneer acknowledges the bid. The man turns to me, winking. Another bid is taken from a woman in a green dress on the other side of the garden. The man next to me gives me a long look, before whispering, "One last shot, hey," as he raises his hand again.

The auctioneer takes the bid, looking to the woman in green for another bid. She seems to consider it, before shaking her head resignedly. In a booming voice the auctioneer calls, "Going once.... Going twice.... Going three times... Sold to the man in the blue shirt."

I turn to the man next to me, who throws his arms around me, lifting me off my feet, spinning me in a full circle...

Lucy is staring at me, her eyes so full of fear that I automatically plaster a smile on my face to show her I am absolutely fine. She looks unconvinced so, without giving it much thought, I throw my arms wide, and envelop her in a hug, similar to the one she just gave me. This seems to have the desired effect of bewildering her even more. I hold onto her for a while, before gently pulling away, thanking her for her kind thoughts. There is no doubt she considers my behaviour odd, but hopefully the weird hug I just gave her will overshadow the memory of my bizarre behaviour beforehand. The last thing I need is her telling Dr. Richmond she is worried about me.

I move past her, and head to the front desk just as Dr. Richmond is coming out of his office with an elderly man. He gives me a warm smile, and while it is definitely still edged with sympathy, it is no longer the overriding emotion present. He informs the gentleman that I will take care of him from here, and goes to retrieve his next patient from the waiting room. By the time the patient has paid and left, there are two more patients in the waiting room. Lucy checks on me a couple of times throughout the morning, but we are too busy for anything more than that.

It is almost two o'clock when Lucy decides to take her break. There is only one person in the waiting room. The appointment book lists him as Mr. Musgrove. I open the waiting room door, inviting him into the nurse's room. He is a tall, middle-aged man, slightly overweight, with a receding hairline. I take his weight, recording it on his card, before offering him a chair. I am seated by the time I go to take his pulse…

I am sitting in a spacious, airy office, facing a younger man, who is seated behind an enormous desk. Huge pieces of art adorn the walls. The man opposite me begins talking.

"John, I know this comes at a difficult time, but I guess there's never a good time for things like this to happen."

"Steven, what are you actually saying?" There is a hint of desperation in his voice.

"John, I don't need to tell you things around here have to change. To that end, the new management has had to make some incredibly tough choices. The decision to let you go was one of the hardest they had to make. I realise things at home have been difficult but…"

He is interrupted when John starts shouting, "Forget what's going on in my personal life! That's got nothing to do with anything. I've been with this company for *nineteen years!*"

*"I* know that, John. *I* understand what you have done for us, but these guys are not looking back, they're looking ahead. The bottom line is they don't see you in the company's future."...

Mr. Musgrove is irritated when I tell him I have to re-inflate the cuff and start again, but he doesn't seem to have registered my mental absence. As I take his blood pressure properly, I wonder what personal problems he was referring to. His blood pressure is 150 over 111. Given what I have just seen, this is really not surprising. I feel awful for him. As I take him back to the waiting room, it amazes me just how oblivious I used to be to all the unhappiness out there.

The last patient on the appointment list is yet to arrive when Lucy finishes her break. I walk out the door only minutes after three. On my way, I pass a well-built, dark-haired man. He looks vaguely familiar. I can't place his face; perhaps I have seen him in the surgery before. I am immensely thankful I won't have to touch him. Something about him makes my skin crawl.

Toby is not outside when I leave the building, so I start walking in the direction he will come from. It is a beautiful autumn afternoon, the sun is shining, and the air is warm without being humid. It isn't long before I see Toby's handsome face looming ahead of me. As soon as he sees me, a smile lights up his face.

"Hey, how was work?" he asks once we have reached each other. His hands are thrust into his pockets. He makes no move to take them out. I am determined not to be outwardly upset, no matter what happens.

"Not bad, thanks. How was rugby?"

"Great! We won, which always helps."

Toby suggests we head towards the beach. This sounds ideal to me, so we make our way to the right stop. Sitting on the bus, it seems as if Toby is making a concerted effort not to get too close to me. Resolved not to become paranoid, I avoid thinking about it, instead asking questions about the game. He fills me in on details, somehow making it sound nothing like the brutal contest I have witnessed in the past.

Once we get there, we buy fish and chips before moving to sit on the grass verge overlooking the beach. From here, we have an uninterrupted view of the promenade stretching the length of the beach, and to the glistening water beyond. The beach is dotted here and there with people soaking up the last of the afternoon sun. Wetsuit-clad surfers paddle about, hoping to catch a decent wave as it rolls in. The promenade is busy with people either strolling or jogging. We talk a little at first, and then eat in silence as we enjoy the view. After a while, Toby launches into what sounds like a prepared speech.

"Juno, there's something I need to talk to you about."

I am prepared for this. I don't want to make it any harder than it obviously already is, so I gently urge him to go on.

"This may sound a little weird, but I've noticed that those dizzy spells you have seem to happen when you touch *me*."

I really thought I was ready to hear anything. I was wrong. This totally throws me. I am speechless for so long that I can see him begin to worry I am having another dizzy spell. In that instant, he looks so deeply concerned that I make a snap decision to come clean. No doubt he will want nothing more to do with me once he knows what a freak I am. Regardless, he deserves an explanation.

"Actually, it doesn't sound weird at all, but what I have to say definitely will. In fact you are probably going to think I am utterly crazy. Please, promise to listen to everything I have to say before judging me."

"Of course I'll listen to you."

He sounds wounded, as though I have somehow offended him. I don't apologise for this. Once he hears what I have to say, he will understand.

"When I woke up in the hospital, I discovered I had developed an ability that I didn't have before."

Toby is looking quizzically at me.

"Basically, whenever I touch somebody for any length of time, I have what I can only call a vision."

Confused he asks, "What sort of vision?"

"Well, it's different for everybody, but basically I think I'm seeing the person's memory. I always see an event that is highly emotive. Sometimes they are very happy scenes, but more often they are terribly sad or frightening moments. It's like I'm actually there, living through it, like an incredibly vivid dream. Only I'm not me, I'm the person whose memory I'm seeing. Generally, once I've seen the memory, I can touch them again and have nothing happen. Does any of that make sense?"

"Not really. I don't understand. What *sort* of things are you seeing?"

"Well, for example, when I touched Izzy for the first time after I got back to school, I was transported back to my mother's funeral. What I witnessed was quite different from my own experience of the day. Instead, I watched the funeral through Izzy's eyes. I saw it the way *she* saw it, from where *she* was sitting. I could even feel her holding Ollie's hand."

"And if you were to touch Izzy now?"

"Nothing. Unless…"

"Unless what?"

"Well, unless between now and when I last touched her she had been through another experience that was very emotional, creating a new memory. Or at least that's how I think it works."

Without warning, I watch as the look on Toby's face changes. It's as though shutters are drawn over his eyes. They remain open, yet there is a veil over them, totally changing his face. It seems now he has closed himself off to me. Fair enough, it is a lot to take in. It is hardly an attribute you would hope for in a girlfriend. Nervous now, I blunder on unthinkingly, hoping somehow to break through his resistance.

"When I touched Sophie, I saw an accident her younger brother had in the park."

This doesn't help. If anything, Toby seems even more withdrawn than before. I decide silence is my best option. Toby won't meet my eyes, so I turn my gaze out to sea. We sit like this for what seems like an age before finally he breaks the silence.

"I suppose you know all about me then." This is said bitterly and suddenly I understand.

"Toby, please believe me when I say I don't know anything about you that you haven't told me yourself! The visions I had when we touched were so strange. It was like nothing really happened at all."

My tone is emphatic. I need to make him understand.

"*Visions? Plural?*"

This is almost shouted at me but I sense his immediate regret. He's not the only one - why on earth did I say visions?

"Well, yes, you are the only person so far I have seen two different memories for, but as I said, they were different from all the others. Nothing really happened in either of them."

"Tell me what you saw."

He is not looking at me. His voice is flat, devoid of all emotion. I would rather he were still shouting at me. Anything would be better than this.

"At first, I saw a hallway. I think it was during the night. A woman in a pink dressing gown walked across the hall, holding a pillow. That's it! There was nothing to it."

Toby has lowered his head, covering his face with both hands. I fight the instinct to touch him. While I am certain of very little, I have no doubt that me touching him is the last thing he wants right now.

I desperately wish I knew what to say to make things better. Sadly, it seems the more I say the worse things become. I revert to silence. When he eventually drops his hands, he keeps his head lowered. In a quietly restrained voice, he asks me to tell him about my second vision. I long to be able to say something that will take away his pain.

I know before speaking that I am only going to exacerbate it, so I say as little as possible.

"I saw a woman in a wheelchair."

He raises his head, and drops it back so he is looking at the sky. I turn away, not wanting to make things even harder.

I watch as a couple no older than us walk hand in hand along the promenade. I imagine for a moment that my life is that simple. I don't know how long we are sitting like this, but eventually I notice that Toby is also staring out at the water.

"It's calming, isn't it?"

"Yes." My voice is barely audible, even to my own ears.

"I'm going to tell you something, Juno, something I haven't told a single soul. It's the reason my Dad and I moved to Sydney."

He continues looking towards the water as he speaks. Not wanting to increase his discomfort, I do the same.

"Before having me, my parents tried for three years to conceive. Finally, they resorted to fertility treatments. I was the result. When I was three, they used fertility drugs again. Mum became pregnant with twins. When she was about half-way through the pregnancy, something went terribly wrong. She ended up delivering two baby boys, who had no chance of survival. It was awful for my parents. I have little memory of that time. All I recall is having an extended stay with my grandparents."

Despite not remembering much himself, Toby's voice sounds despondent.

"After that, they decided I was enough, they were happy to call it quits. Then, just over a year ago, Mum found out she was pregnant again. It was totally unexpected. She was 44 years old. Never before had she been able to conceive naturally. For years, they had dreamed of another baby, suddenly, out of the blue, their wish was being granted. It took me a while to get used to the idea. By the time the baby was due, we were all really excited.

"Due to her age, and what she had previously been through, she had to have loads of tests. We found out quite early on she was having a girl. Dad and I spent whatever spare time we had, converting the guest bedroom into a nursery. Dad's amazing with his hands, Juno. He paints beautifully. He even carves wood. Mum was never allowed into the room. We kept it as a surprise, revealing the completed room to her on Christmas Day. It was so beautiful Juno, Mum was thrilled with it. We were all so happy then.

"Just after Christmas, Mum gave birth to a healthy baby girl. She was absolutely perfect and we named her Rebecca."

He pauses. When I glance at him briefly I can see he is fighting back tears. I look away again, waiting until he is ready to go on.

"At first, things seemed fine. To be honest, I was so busy with school, and cricket, I wasn't much help to Mum. Dad was at work a lot, because they were working on a big case. There was some problem with breast-feeding. Mum switched to the bottle, which we hoped would make things easier on her. She was definitely exhausted. Dad and I were worried about her, but we just assumed this was the hard part - that things would get better.

"But things didn't get better, they got worse. Dad and I did what we could. Between us, we did the shopping, cooking and cleaning. None of it made any difference. It didn't seem to help Mum at all. She stopped getting dressed and started staying in her pyjamas all day long. She barely ate. She no longer seemed interested in anything, least of all Rebecca. She seemed to do nothing but sleep. Several times I came home from school to find Rebecca hysterical in her cot, Mum asleep in her bed. I was worried about her, Juno, but I was also angry. It didn't seem fair to Rebecca. I couldn't understand it. She had been so desperate for a baby for so long, and finally when she had the one thing she had always wanted, she didn't seem to want it any more.

"In order to take the pressure off Mum, Dad hired a nurse to help during the days. He had our family doctor come to the house to see her. The doctor examined her, but he couldn't get through to her any more than we could. He said she was suffering from post-natal depression. He told us she needed to see a psychiatrist, who would be better equipped at handling these sorts of cases. He gave us a referral. Dad booked the first available appointment, for the following Monday. Dad arranged to take the morning off work so he could go with her. About two am that Monday morning, I heard Rebecca crying. I got out of bed in case Mum wasn't going to. Before I'd walked out of my room, I saw Mum walking across the hall into Rebecca's room."

This is clearly the memory I witnessed.

"When Mum was pregnant with me, Dad built her a rocking chair. After the twins died, they gave it away. As soon as

Mum was through her first trimester, he started making a new one. He wanted Mum to be able to sit and feed the baby comfortably. I saw she had a pillow with her and assumed it was to put behind her back on the chair. I'd seen her do that before."

His tone is almost pleading now, imploring me to believe him. I say nothing, nervous about making things worse. Instead, I use my eyes to show him I understand.

"I went back to bed."

His voice catches here. I know what's coming. I can't bear for him to have to continue talking, but I understand the need for him to finally say it out loud.

"I could have stopped her, Juno, but I didn't. Rebecca would still be alive if I'd only stopped her."

He is no longer able to hold back the tears. I am unable to stop myself from moving towards him, putting my arms around him. My own experience tells me there's no point talking to him. I need to let him cry it out, before trying to comfort him. What a horrible thing to have happened. He must have played that scene over and over in his mind. When it actually happened, it caused little if any emotion, explaining why what I saw confused me. I assume each time the scene was repeated in his head, the emotions attached to it increased in intensity.

Toby and I have both been walking around weighed down by shameful secrets we were too scared to share. Hopefully, by unburdening ourselves, our loads will be lighter to bear. I hold him while he weeps. It takes time but gradually he becomes quieter until finally he is silent. I dig a packet of tissues out of my bag, handing them to him. He looks at me through tear-stained eyes. I am consoled, as looking into his eyes, I see the shadow is gone, leaving behind the Toby I know. When it feels as though he is calmer, I start talking.

"Toby, you have to know that what happened wasn't your fault. You assumed what anybody under the circumstances would have."

"But I *knew* how unhappy she was. I *knew* she wasn't behaving normally. I *knew* she was sick."

"But you *couldn't* have known what she was going to do. It's more than likely that even *she* didn't know what she was going to do until it happened."

This is clearly a possibility he hasn't considered until now. Somehow it seems to shift things a little.

"Do you really think that's possible?"

"Absolutely! Clearly, she was seriously unwell. Her thoughts would have been all over the place. You said yourself she wasn't well enough to get dressed, let alone cook or clean. It's doubtful she was capable of devising any kind of plan, no matter how simple."

He is looking at me, his eyes filled with gratitude. I am so pleased to have been able to alleviate his pain, even momentarily.

"She was ultimately diagnosed with a major postpartum psychosis, and judged unfit to stand trial. She was admitted to a psychiatric facility in Melbourne. With Mum and Rebecca both gone, the house felt like a mausoleum. Dad and I couldn't face going into Rebecca's room. Dad started sleeping on the couch rather than in his and Mum's bedroom; I started having nightmares, waking around two every morning. It was as though I was re-living that time, over and over, in a desperate attempt to change the way things turned out, to create a happy ending.

"Eventually, Dad decided we needed a complete change. He did some research and found a psychiatric clinic in Sydney, which specialised in postpartum psychosis. Once we secured a place for Mum, Dad applied for a transfer, which was successful. It sounds strange, but it's easier being here where nobody knows what happened. At times, it is almost as though it *hasn't* happened.

"The reason I was late to school on Tuesday for our drama performance was because I was going to visit her in the new place for the first time. Her condition has worsened to the point where she's catatonic. If the staff didn't move her, she would spend all day in bed. As it is, she spends her day sitting in a wheel-chair, not talking or even moving. It's as though her spirit has left her body completely."

The sun slips below the horizon. The temperature has dropped. All of a sudden, it is quite cool. I wrap my arms around myself to keep warm. Toby notices and puts his arms around me, pulling me close. I rest my head on his shoulder. We sit in comfortable silence. When it is totally dark, we walk back to the bus stop, his arm still around my shoulders. It has been such an incredibly sad afternoon. Strangely, I am left feeling more peaceful than I have in weeks.

I am home just before seven. Dad is reading on the couch. I don't ask him whether Rosie called. I don't have to.

# Chapter 26

The heady scent of gardenia hangs in the air. I am holding a bunch of them. The cream petals look as soft as velvet against the gleaming green leaves. Mum is standing before me, looking ethereal. She smiles at me, reaching her hands out to accept the flowers. As I raise my hands to give them to her, the petals begin to wither and discolour, until I am holding nothing but handfuls of ash. I look to Mum. She is no longer there.

A year ago today, Rosie, Mum, Dad and I shared a sumptuous seafood lunch, overlooking the water, before an afternoon stroll along the beach. Later at home, we presented Rosie with a collector's edition of her favourite movie, *South Pacific*. Dad and I gave Mum a voucher for a day at a luxury spa. This year's Mother's Day will be so starkly different, it is almost impossible to comprehend. Mum is gone from our lives; Rosie is in a home. It is more than likely she won't even recognise us today.

The drive to Greenfields is a quiet one. When Rosie misses a Saturday night phone call, it invariably means Sunday will not be a great day. The best we can hope for is that she will be with us, but enormously tired, not up for much in the way of either conversation or activity. The weather can't seem to make up its mind. The sky above us is blue, with fluffy white clouds. In the distance, dark grey clouds hover menacingly.

My mind keeps returning to Toby. I keep thinking about what he and his family are going through. If I hadn't heard it from his very mouth, I would never have believed he was mourning the way he is. Outwardly, he seems like the happiest, most carefree boy in the world. In contrast, I walk around with the weight of the world on my shoulders. I may as well have the word 'GRIEVING' tattooed on my forehead. I wonder if I found myself in a totally different environment, surrounded by people who were unaware of Mum's accident, would I be able to behave as though nothing had happened?

Rosie is in her room when we arrive. She is very happy to see us, although who she actually thinks we are isn't clear. The nurse sitting with her gets up to go. We pull up seats by the bed. She is cheerful and lively. Even though she isn't the Rosie we know and love, it is far easier to see her like this than withdrawn, suspicious and uncommunicative. I am reminded of Toby's mum, sitting mute and lifeless in her wheelchair. I miss Mum more than words can express. If I had the choice to bring her back now, but to have her be the way Toby's mum is, I honestly don't know if I would.

Rosie is lying on her bed, her upper body elevated by a tilt in the bed and a surplus of pillows. She is animatedly pointing to a section of the ceiling, asking us to share the beautiful view from the porthole of her ship's cabin. As she describes the colourful fish she can see, Dad and I ooh and aah appreciatively. Occasionally, something other than a fish is spotted. Rosie points excitedly, as she chronicles the passing parade of sea life.

She recounts a story about a child on board, who was behaving badly. Rosie told the young girl off. Later, Rosie herself was scolded for berating the child so loudly that she woke other passengers who were resting. She giggles like a child herself, as she recalls how she made a sincere apology to the passengers and crew later that day. I have no idea if Rosie is reliving a memory from her past, or whether this is just a symptom of her illness. It makes little difference either way. She is happy, nothing else matters.

We know better than to ask questions as they can cause her to become confused, even distressed. Instead we sit contentedly sharing her illusion. Not long after midday, a nurse comes in to feed her. Dad and I prepare to leave. Rosie takes hold of my hand in both of hers. She looks deeply into my eyes and thanks me warmly for coming.

"Do be sure to come back and visit me soon."

As she says this, she squeezes my hand a little tighter. For one brief moment, I know I am looking at my Rosie, and then she is gone again. That will have to be enough for me to hold onto for now.

We emerge out of Greenfields to find the weather has finally made up its mind. The sky is a glorious blue, with only soft, billowy clouds visible. There is a gentle breeze blowing. As we climb into the car, we roll down the windows to enjoy it. Dad starts the car, while I select a CD from the glove box. Before long, the two of us are humming along to Jason Mraz.

I am in my room studying for a biology test when Toby calls. He asks how my day was. I tell him a bit about Rosie. Things between us have changed again. Knowing what I now do, I find myself carefully censoring the things I say. I guess that's only natural. I imagine that as time goes by this will become easier. We talk a little about yesterday. He thanks me for being there for him. I tell him the feeling is mutual and that it goes without saying we will keep each other's confidences. He seems subdued, and while I am not happy about it, I am glad he no longer feels the need for pretence. He can drop his mask; he can be himself, at least with me.

# Chapter 27

Through closed lids, I can feel the sun's rays on my face. Opening my eyes, I find myself in a field of wheat, slender stalks as tall as I am, gently swaying in the wind. With outstretched arms, I turn slowly in a full circle, feeling the stalks brush against my skin. Gradually, I become aware of Mum's voice calling me. I stop turning and look around for her. She says my name again. I start moving towards the sound of her voice.

"Juno."

"I'm coming," I call, moving in the direction of her voice.

"Juno."

"Mum? Where are you? I can't see you."

I am walking faster now, sweeping the wheat out of my path as I search for her.

"I'm here, Juno."

The wheat seems to be growing taller and denser.

"It's ok, Juno."

"Mum, wait for me, I'm coming!"

Panic is now discernible in my voice.

"It's ok, darling."

Her voice now sounds as if it's coming from a distance.

"Please wait for me, please, please."

There is no response. Desperately crying now, I run, batting the stalks out of my path. I trip and stumble to the ground.

The dream wasn't real. The tears on my cheeks are. I roll over, staring at her face until the tears dry, and my racing heart slows to normal. My alarm rings. I switch it off and get out of bed. Once I am showered and dressed, I go to have breakfast.

The routine school provides is both comforting, and terrifying. It means that most of the time, I know where I need to be, what I need to be doing. It also means hours, days and weeks pass by, constantly taking me further away from the time she was here with us.

When Sophie gets on the bus she is eager to know if I have had any new experiences. Her interest is genuine. Hesitantly, I tell her about witnessing the unfortunate man being made redundant. Sophie is highly sensitive. I can see she feels awful just hearing about it. I hope this will help her to understand that, most of the time, my visions are anything but exciting.

She explains she spent much of yesterday, surfing the Internet, looking for information on this kind of thing. Apparently, there is a wealth of material about reading people's minds, but absolutely nothing about reading people's memories. For some reason, this conversation makes me uncomfortable. I experience an uncharacteristic flash of anger towards Sophie. The whole situation still feels so raw, so personal, so connected with what happened to Mum.

Normally, I have to explain nothing to Sophie. She generally understands my thought processes often better than I do. Today, she seems oblivious, stubbornly determined to continue hounding me about the Gift. I attempt to keep my irritation in check. My reticence to continue the conversation is soon obvious. Reluctantly, she changes the subject, asking how Saturday night with Toby was. I tell her only that we sorted things out, and are back on track. She is truly pleased for me. Once we are off the bus, we head straight to biology, spending the time before the bell quizzing each other in preparation for the test.

Toby is waiting for me outside maths class. His smile is different now, not as big but somehow more authentic. He opens the door for me. We make our way into the classroom. The lesson is on trigonometric ratios. I am lost before we even start. Toby intuits my frustration. He whispers for me not to worry as he will explain it all later. As soon as we are out of class, Toby takes my hand, suggesting we get together one afternoon to go over the trig. I agree, adding that perhaps he could stay for dinner to meet my Dad. I regret it almost as soon as it is out of my mouth, but the huge grin on his face reassures me I need not have.

In double English, we are looking at the themes of crime, guilt, and innocence in *Great Expectations*. Mrs. Samuels is an extraordinary teacher. She has a way of imparting huge amounts of knowledge, without lecturing. Rather than spoon-feeding facts, she deftly drops subtle clues, leading the class on a journey that inevitably winds up just where we need to be. There is something empowering about this method of teaching. You end up feeling as though you have achieved something.

I spot Piper a few metres ahead of me in the hallway. I am right behind her by the time we walk into history. I stare intently at the back of her neck, looking for evidence of the bird tattoo. I think I can see a small black mark, but her shirt collar is too high for me to see anything more. She walks towards the rear of the classroom. I follow her, sitting in the seat next to hers. Our eyes meet. I smile cautiously, receiving a guarded smile in return. This is the most we have ever interacted; I find myself wondering if her knowledge of Mum's passing has softened her attitude towards me.

As the teacher begins to address us, Piper folds her arms on the table in front of her, knowing as we all do, it will be sometime before anything noteworthy comes out of his mouth. If only he were more like Mrs. Samuels. World War II might actually be thought-provoking rather than soul-destroying.

I too place my folded arms on the desk. After a few minutes, without giving it much thought, I surreptitiously move my left elbow in tiny increments towards Piper's. I feel like a voyeur. Since getting a glimpse into her other world, I am intrigued by Piper, keen to know more. I don't need to look to know when my elbow is touching hers...

I am no longer in history class. Instead, I am in the public gallery of a courtroom, sitting in the second row. The courtroom is full. Standing in front and to the right of me is a slender, tall, red-haired woman. I am startled by a booming voice.

"Ladies and gentlemen of the jury, have you reached a verdict upon which you are all agreed?"

The judge is facing the jury. One juror, a middle-aged man, stands while the rest remain seated.

"We have, your Honor," answers the appointed juror.

"How do you find the defendant?"

"We, the jury, find the defendant guilty of manslaughter as charged in the indictment."

As these words are spoken I feel Piper's body collapse in on itself ...

I am back in the classroom. Piper is sitting back in her chair, arms folded across her chest. I avoid looking at her for the rest of the class, concerned she might have been made uncomfortable by my touch.

It is still raining steadily. Normally, we would go to the gym but Toby and I decide to eat in the cafeteria. Conversation doesn't flow quite as quickly as before. Looking back, I wonder how much of an effort that was for him. I guess anyone arriving at a new school, faced with a lot of potential new friends, will endeavour to make as positive an impression as possible. He is definitely quieter now, noticeably more relaxed, not only in himself but also with me.

"It's still raining out there," he says, glancing out the window after we have eaten. "How about we tackle that trig now so that you have it sorted before tomorrow's class?"

"That would be great", I reply, removing my maths books from my bag. Perhaps the idea of dinner with Dad was rushing things a little.

Toby begins explaining the idea of trigonometric ratios. He describes things so simply, answers my questions so succinctly, that by the time we are finished, I wonder out loud how on earth I was so confused in the first place.

"I think just the sight of equations sends many people into a frenzy, effectively ruling out any possibility of learning."

He says this kindly, without even the hint of a smile.

"Sadly, I think I am one of those people," I reply with a laugh.

"At least now when I come for dinner we won't have to worry about homework, we can just enjoy ourselves."

Relief at this last comment courses through me. I really need to stop being so paranoid.

Hearing my key in the door, Astrid makes her way to the hallway. She is a tiny woman, with dark hair worn short. She has a large black beauty spot on her round face. She wears an apron, and is clutching both sides of it in her hands, nervously working the fabric between her fingers. She is a reserved woman, not one to push herself on others. It would be easy for me to avoid touching her altogether but seeing her serious, sad eyes fill with tears, I am compelled to go to her, wrapping my arms around her. She welcomes my hug...

Immediately, I am sitting on a hard straight-backed chair in a darkened, airless bedroom. The blinds are drawn shut. The only light in the room comes from a small bedside lamp with a fringed shade. In the bed lies the withered figure of a woman. Her pallor is sallow, almost the same colour as the sheets on which she lies. The only medical equipment in the room is an intravenous drip next to the bed. The woman appears to be barely breathing. Suddenly there is one loud shuddering inhalation, followed by a long wheezing sound, almost like the sound of air rushing out of a punctured tyre. Then there is nothing…

I am back in my hallway. I gently release Astrid from my grip. We swap condolences and together make our way to the kitchen.

The place looks beautifully clean, and the smells wafting from the kitchen are fabulous. Astrid has been busy. There is a fresh batch of scones on the kitchen counter. I make us both a cup of tea, while she gets out the cream and jam. We each have a scone, drink tea and talk about Rosie. Astrid seems to love her almost as much as I do, which immediately deepens my respect for her. Astrid mentions she visited Rosie yesterday afternoon, arriving immediately after she had been fed lunch. We must have just missed each other. Rosie was still enjoying her time on board the ship. Astrid was treated to a similar portrayal of life through the porthole.

Once we have finished our scones, Astrid asks me to help her create a monthly meal plan for our dinners. She tells me it will be a big help to her when shopping to know in advance what meals she will be making. She has brought along some cookbooks. Together we flip through them, selecting a month's worth of meals. She has chosen honey soy chicken for tonight's dinner, which I assure her will be a big hit.

I do my trig homework and find, thanks to Toby, it is not too hard at all. Astrid is ready to leave just as Dad is arriving home. Over dinner I mention the possibility of Toby joining us one night. Dad reacts enthusiastically. We decide Thursday is the best night. Neither of us mentions the time, or the fact Rosie hasn't called.

As I lay in bed, I mull over Piper's memory. While I can't be totally sure, I have a strong intuition that she is closely related to the woman I saw standing trial. If I was to hazard a guess, I would suggest it was her mother. The skin tone, body frame and hair colour of the woman was almost identical to Piper's. The most striking similarity though was the long, regal neck. Although I couldn't see her face, something about her gave me the sense that she was older. If I'm right, Piper's mother is behind bars somewhere. Could that be the reason she changed schools this year? If nothing else, the Gift has taught me just how complicated people's lives can be.

# Chapter 28

I am woken by the sound of the phone ringing. Climbing out of bed, I walk into the living room to answer the call.

"Hello, Juno speaking."

"Juno, darling, it's Mum."

Her voice is clear and strong, as though she is right in the room with me.

"Mum? Mum? Where are you?"

"I'm here, Juno."

Still holding the phone to my ear I turn, looking all around the room.

"Where? I can't see you."

"I'm right here, darling."

"But you're not here, Mum! I'm looking everywhere, and I can't find you. You aren't here! Mum? Why aren't you here? Please? Mum?"

"I am here, Juno, I'm right here, I'm with you."

Her voice sounds a little quieter now. There is the faint sound of static on the line.

"Where? You're not here! Where are you?"

I am almost shouting into the telephone now, clutching the phone desperately to my ear. Distraught now, I turn left and right, searching for a sign of her.

"I am here, Juno, right here, where I've always been. I'm always here, always with you. I love you, Juno."

Her voice can barely be heard through the static, which grows louder by the second.

"Please don't go! Don't leave me! Mum? Mum?"

I am sobbing. There is only static now, so loud I have to hold the phone away from my ear.

"I love you, Mum."

This is cried to an empty room.

My hammering heart is all I can hear as I lay staring at the ceiling. The dreams when I can hear her but not see her are the hardest to cope with. Is it significant that I am hearing her disembodied voice? The thought that I am losing the ability to remember her face, to picture it in my mind's eye, petrifies me. I turn to stare at her photo again. I want to burn the image onto my retinas, sear it into my brain to last for eternity.

During breakfast, Dad and I make arrangements to meet after school so we can drive to the counselling session together. Although I am not looking forward to it, I am dreading it far less than the previous session. Talking to Sylvia was far easier than I had anticipated.

I share my concerns about my most recent dreams with Sophie. Rather than focusing on the fact that I can't see Mum's face, she is eager to know what Mum's voice says in the dreams.

> "She just keeps saying 'I'm here, I'm with you', but I am never able to see her."

Sophie's face lights up. She smiles knowingly, before confidently asserting that the message Mum is trying to communicate to me is very clear.

> "She *is* here. She is *with* you, at *all* times. Even though you can't see her. She wants you to rest easy in the knowledge that her spirit is with you *always*."

There is not a shred of doubt in my mind that Sophie is speaking the truth, but it is her truth. While I appreciate the sentiment, and would like nothing more than to share her conviction, Sophie is hardly an expert in dream interpretation. Regardless, my anxiety is caused not by the words Mum speaks in my dreams, but by the fact that I can't see her face. Perhaps my sub-conscious mind is punishing me for causing her accident, by obliterating my memory of her face.

"Can you please just look into the whole disembodied voice thing for me?" I ask, the pleading tone in my voice surprising even me. She vows to do it. I know she will, although I can sense she is frustrated with herself at not being able to persuade me to come around to her way of thinking.

Toby is waiting for me outside the main building, smiling warmly as he reaches for my hand. I invite him for dinner on Thursday night and he readily accepts.

"Is there anything you don't eat?"

"Mmmm, only marzipan," he says with a smile.

"Gee," I reply jokingly, "that's going to be a hard one to work around."

We sit side by side in class. I am relieved to find today's lesson far more intelligible than yesterday's. He smiles encouragingly at me as I successfully calculate secants, cosecants and cotangents.

As I enter history class, I scan the room for Piper. She is sitting alone. I intentionally sit somewhere else. I have no idea if she noticed my arm touching hers yesterday and reacted or if she just sat back when she did because she felt like it. In case it was the former, and she is now wary of me, I have decided to leave her alone for a while. Given what I saw yesterday, I imagine she has enough to deal with right now.

We have double drama to finish the day. We continue working in our groups of four. My group has one other girl named Lauren and two boys named Nick and Dominic. They are all relatively easy to work with. Before long, we are brainstorming some great ideas about how we can best depict bullying. I contribute as much as I can; however, the closer we come to the end of the lesson, the more my thoughts stray to the upcoming counselling session.

Dad is smiling at me as I make my way to the car. He asks about my day, but seems preoccupied, probably as nervous as I am about the session. The waiting room is empty when we arrive. The receptionist is on the phone. She smiles, gesturing to the door behind her and indicating for us to go in. Dad knocks lightly, before opening the door to let me in. Sylvia welcomes us both. We sit side by side on the couch. Today she is wearing a form-fitting, leopard-print top over dark denim jeans, with camel-coloured, knee-high boots. She has a deep green scarf knotted at her neck. Large gold earrings in the shape of peace signs dangle from her ears.

Having seated herself in an armchair opposite us, Sylvia wastes no time at all, immediately announcing to Dad that I have something important to tell him. I have no idea what she is referring to. It must have something to do with the one-sided conversation we had at the end of our first session. I look at her apologetically, hoping this will be enough. She smiles genuinely at me before winking conspiratorially, as though we are accomplices in some secret plot. She then calmly proceeds to tell Dad that I have convinced myself I am to blame for Mum's death. I am rendered speechless. What happened to patient confidentiality?

"What? I don't understand, Juno. Why would you think that?"

Dad sounds more mystified than angry. Sylvia looks at me expectantly, as though I am supposed to provide him with an answer. I can't even look at him, and am still too stunned to speak. I hang my head, gazing at my hands in my lap. I can't believe this is happening. I will the floor to open up and swallow me whole. When I fail to respond, Sylvia goes on. She tells Dad everything, including the phone call I made to Lily, sparing no detail whatsoever.

I feel utterly betrayed and bereft, not to mention terrified, wondering how Dad will react to this information. I feel his eyes on me. I am frightened to face him but I force myself. The sadness in his eyes is so enormous that the guilt I have recently begun to manage quite well looms over me like an enormous teetering wall, ready to crush me under its weight. I expect anger, rejection, even hatred. When he reaches out for me, putting his arms around me, I am completely disconcerted. He is holding me, hugging me to him, crying.

"It wasn't your fault, Juno. Sometimes bad things just happen. Even if she had been going to collect your dress, it still wouldn't have been your fault."

It takes a few moments for me to process what I have just heard. When I finally do, I am so startled that I react bodily, jerking backwards. My arms are now extended in front of me so I am able to look at him.

"What do you mean 'Even if' she had been going to get my dress?" I ask, quietly.

"Oh, Juno, your dress was already in the car when the accident happened. She must have collected it earlier in the day, probably right after you called her. The accident happened about five hundred metres from Juno's, nowhere near the dry cleaners."

The enormity of what I am hearing is too much to sink in. I feel totally numb but it is a far better feeling than the crushing guilt of moments ago.

Dad wraps his arms around me again, and I realise this is the closest we have been physically since I started back at school. He keeps one arm around my shoulders and, with his free hand, he takes hold of one of mine. Looking at both of us intently, Sylvia says,

"Together you have suffered a loss so catastrophic that, understandably, it has caused you both to lose your footing. Under circumstances like these, it is easy to imagine that this loss is the only thing binding the two of you together. It is important that you both know that this couldn't be further from the truth. Having met and spoken with each of you individually, I can assure you that between the two of you there is an incredibly deep and mutual love and abiding respect for one another." At this, Dad gives my hand a squeeze.

"Obviously, I never met Lily, but having listened to the two of you talk about her, I understand that she was loving, generous of spirit and affectionate. You have both described a woman who was spontaneous, gregarious and vivacious. The two of you adored her for all these things. With Lily as the centrepiece of your lives, you were destined to experience life in a certain way. The years of memories you have can *never* be taken from you. They need to be cherished and treasured. Remembering happier times now will inevitably be painful. However, as time goes by the intensity of this pain will gradually lessen."

This is one of my greatest fears. It destroys me to think that one day I will be able to think about Mum, and not ache. Perhaps in response to the look on my face, Sylvia goes on.

"The hurt will never disappear altogether, but it will eventually become less difficult to live with. The sadness becomes something precious. Something you tuck away, like a priceless jewel in your pocket; one you touch often to see if it is still there.

"In terms of personality types, you are both very different to Lily. The two of you are in fact very much alike. The dynamic that existed between the three of you was, by all accounts, wonderful. The situation you are left with now is a very different one but, in time, it will be equally as magnificent in its own way. Until then, you will have to go through a period of adjustment. This is going to take some time. The most important thing right now is that you communicate with one another."

Pointedly looking at me, she adds, "We have seen just now how not communicating openly with one another can create harmful misunderstandings." As I turn to look at Dad, he leans forward and places a kiss on my forehead. Being able to look at him, to be able to acknowledge his suffering but not feel responsible for it, is very liberating. I smile, before turning to Sylvia, nodding for her to go on.

"In order to help with this adjustment, I want the two of you to start creating new memories together so I am prescribing weekly date nights. Together you need to choose a night that works for you both, and commit to spending that night together every week. You must go out somewhere, be it to a movie, bowling, the museum, a restaurant or even a walk around the park. A night at home does not count. If for some reason you miss a date night, you must agree to re-schedule for another night that same week. Agreed?"

We both concur, and Sylvia produces a piece of paper printed with the details she just outlined. She has made three copies, and asks us both to sign and date each one. She presents both of us with a copy, and keeps the third.

"I also want you to talk about Lily whenever you feel like it and, more importantly, even when you don't. It will be painful - there is no getting away from that - but you must not avoid the pain. There is nothing more harmful you can do right now than suppress your feelings. They need to be felt. They need expression. Repressing them will only lead to bigger problems down the line."

She talks a little more about the grieving process in general, outlining the different stages we might expect to experience. The first stage is shock and denial, and Sylvia believes that we have probably both moved through this. The next stage is pain and guilt, and we are all in agreement that this is the stage we are dealing with at the moment. She explains that, as time progresses, we may find ourselves lashing out in anger, most likely directed towards each other, or those closest to us. This is hard to take in, and rather than continue with the lecture, Sylvia simply gives us both copies of a pamphlet that covers much of what she has been talking about. She suggests that it might prove useful at some point in the future. After agreeing to come back together in a month's time, we are free to go.

Dad and I are still holding hands when we emerge from the building onto the street. The late afternoon sun is hanging low in the sky, which is tinted a beautiful mixture of pink and orange. I feel lighter than I have in weeks, and this seems to positively affect Dad too. We walk to the car, and decide that tomorrow night will be our first date night.

Although conversation doesn't exactly flow at dinner, there is definitely a more pronounced feeling of ease between us. We talk a little about our session with Sylvia. Dad is still upset that I have been blaming myself this whole time, and wants to understand why I didn't talk to him about it. I try to explain that I was terrified he would never be able to forgive me if he knew Mum had died because I'd only been thinking about myself. Yet again I am crying, and Dad is up and out of his seat hugging me.

"Juno, darling, you have to know that there is *absolutely nothing* you could ever tell me that would be unforgivable, nothing you could say that would ever stop me from loving you more than anything in the world."

It is almost seven o'clock before I realise the time. It seems that the stretches of Rosie's bad days are getting longer, but I try not to dwell on this thought. Despite having not had a single experience today, the emotional release during the session with Sylvia is enough to have wiped me out, and I am asleep within minutes of my head hitting the pillow.

# Chapter 29

M y arms are behind me, dragging something heavy. I know without looking that I am pulling a wheel-barrow, laden with stones. Ahead of me is a steep hill. Just looking at it makes me enormously weary. As I start up the hill, I find every step a struggle. The crest is so far away. It appears to be unreachable. I avert my gaze to the road just in front of me. This way, I am not looking too far ahead. I can take the hill one step at a time.

"Juno!"

Mum calls to me. Automatically, my gaze lifts. There she stands at the top of the hill, which is definitely closer now. She looks so real, so solid. I don't want to take my eyes off her. I am determined to reach her. I pull harder, leaning heavily into the incline, trying to increase my pace, all the while gazing at her smiling face. The higher I climb, the heavier the barrow seems to become. My legs are aching. The muscles in my arms are straining, with the massive effort required to move.

"Juno, let it go."

As she says this, she spreads her arms wide, as though waiting for me to run into them. I hesitate, not sure what I am supposed to do.

"Let it go, darling. It's not yours to carry any more. You can let it go now."

I understand what she wants from me yet, for some reason, I am loath to do it. It seems I have become attached to my burden. Reluctantly, I drag my gaze away from her, looking over my shoulder. The wheelbarrow is immense. Gigantic boulders are piled high on top of one another. Looking at the huge load I am carrying, my decision is made a little easier. Slowly, I release my grip on one handle, then the other. I stand still, watching as the barrow rolls down the hill, picking up speed before careening off the edge, out into the unknown. I feel so amazingly light, like I could float the rest of the way up the hill. Smiling, I turn back towards her - only to find she has vanished.

I wake crying. I give into it, allowing the tears to come as I bury my face into the pillow. Sylvia's words about not suppressing my feelings ring in my ears. The agony of losing Mum is one thing. As horrible as it feels, it is easier to accept than the pointless self-pity that seems to accompany it. I try to ignore these unwelcome thoughts as they enter my mind.

The smell of coffee brewing drifts in the air as I enter the kitchen. Dad greets me taking crumpets out of the toaster and slathering them in butter. He places two on a plate in front of me, next to a jar of Vegemite. I thank him and apply the Vegemite sparingly, mesmerised by the butter melting into the pits of the crumpet. Between mouthfuls, I ask,

"So, where do you think we should go tonight?"

"I have everything under control. All *you* need to do is come home straight after school."

"Where are we going?"

"It's a surprise!"

This is said with a satisfied grin. I'm not a big one for surprises, however, seeing Dad this happy, I am definitely not going to put up a fight.

"Oh, and I've left a note for Astrid letting her know we won't need dinner tonight, but that we will need dinner for three tomorrow. Is there anything special you would like her to cook?"

"So long as you're not cooking, anything will be fine," I retort cheekily, which earns me a look of mock horror.

Sophie looks like the proverbial cat having swallowed the world's largest canary. Even before she has taken her seat on the bus she has excitedly started to tell me what she has uncovered about my dreams.

"Firstly, seeing wheat fields in a dream symbolises resurrection or reincarnation!"

Sophie's face lights up as she says this. As I am yet to hear anything remotely relating to me, I look at her blankly. Hardly discouraged, she continues.

"To dream you are having a telephone conversation with someone you know means there is something important you need to discuss with that person. This issue may have to do with letting go of something, possibly some part of yourself."

Sophie must read something on my face because she pauses here. My skin has broken out in tiny goose bumps all over. The hairs on my arms and legs are raised. She looks at me searchingly. I am not prepared to share my most recent dream, so I remain mute.

"Is there anything else?" I ask even though it is abundantly clear she has more to say.

"Yes, and I left the best for last. The thing about dream interpretation is that often the same dream can have multiple meanings depending on where you look."

I nod in understanding, wanting her to hurry up and get to the point.

"However, when it comes to hearing voices in dreams, almost every reference I found said exactly the same thing."

Her elation is so evident it is hard not to be affected by it.

"So, are you going to tell me? Or are you going to keep me guessing?"

She is seriously enjoying herself now.

"Ok, are you ready for this?"

"Come on, you're driving me nuts," I groan.

"A disembodied voice in a dream is *always* a guide or guardian angel. If you can remember what the voice says, you should follow their advice. They are infallible. So you see, Juno, I was right! Lily's trying to tell you she's still with you. She's become one of your spirit guides. She's watching over you, to help you. You need to start believing."

The goose bumps are back. Tears are welling in my eyes. Sophie is delighted to see her words have had an effect on me. She takes my hand in hers and lays her head on my shoulder. I gaze out the bus window, seeing nothing. Against my better judgement, I find I am beginning to think there might actually be something to what Sophie is saying.

Sophie senses she has made some headway so there is no stopping her. As we alight from the bus, she chats animatedly about all the books she wants me to read. She tells me about the Reiki course she is doing, suggesting I might find it interesting. Her passion is genuine. I am more than a little overwhelmed, which Sophie is sensitive enough to notice. Without discussing it, we head straight to chemistry, skipping the morning's field session.

I have physics next. As I walk into class, Ollie bounds up behind me. We sit next to each other near the back of the room. Many people are still walking on eggshells around me. Ollie's treatment of me is totally unchanged. It is powerfully refreshing.

"How are you doing, Juno?" he asks training his full attention on me.

"It's really hard, Ollie, but I'm coping."

"What about your Dad? How's he going?"

"To be honest, Ollie, we haven't been talking about it much. Up till now we've been dealing with things kind of separately. We haven't exactly been ignoring what's happened. How could we? It's more that we have avoided directly talking about it. I guess it hurts so much already that we have both been shying away from causing each other any extra pain. Does that make sense?"

"It sure does. I guess there's no right or wrong way. You have to find what works for the two of you."

"Well, we've just started seeing a grief counsellor. It's not that we have been doing the wrong thing, but she does believe we need to connect more. Basically, we need to stop dodging the painful stuff. We're working on it. Hopefully, things will be better going forward."

"Good for you," he says, lavishing me with a warm smile just as the teacher arrives.

I am already seated in history when Piper enters, taking the seat next to mine. Hopefully this indicates that she didn't notice anything strange about my behaviour on Monday. I am careful not to touch her, concerned that she doesn't think I'm creepy. I am also conscious of not being too obvious about it. The teacher starts droning on about the League of Nations. I do my best to pay attention.

As the bell goes signalling the end of the day, Toby and I walk out of maths into the hallway.

"Date night tonight, huh?" he asks as he takes my hand.

"Yeah, tonight's the night."

"What are the two of you going to do?"

"No idea. Dad is surprising me, which is a little scary."

We have reached the end of the hallway. As we start down the stairs, he says, "Well, have a great night, wherever you go. I look forward to hearing all about it tomorrow."

He gives my hand a squeeze and walks off, stopping to turn and wave before rounding the corner. Sophie is soon by my side and we walk to the bus stop.

Dad is home early from work. He is dressed casually in jeans and a t-shirt. I shower, dressing similarly, and am ready to go. I am still in the dark as to our destination.

"So, any plans to put me out of my misery?"

"Not a chance," he says, laughing and handing me a piece of material.

"Put this on."

"What is it?" I ask, turning it over in my hands?

"A blindfold," he replies, grinning widely.

"Dad! You can't be serious?"

"Never more so."

He opens the car door for me. Once I am belted into the front seat, he ties the blindfold around my head, before hopping into the driver's seat. Dad puts on an Oasis CD. Very soon, we are both singing along. Mum's favourite Oasis song is *Electric*. When it comes on, we both join in for the chorus at the top of our voices. It feels great. With my eyes closed, I can almost imagine she is here with us, singing along too.

As the CD finishes, we are still driving. After a brief silence, Dad starts talking.

"For our first anniversary, your Mum blindfolded me. She walked me in circles until I was so disoriented I had no idea where I was. She led me on a thirty-minute walk. When we finally stopped, she took off the blindfold. We were in McKell Park, standing at the exact spot where we were married. Rosie had waited until we arrived. I just caught a glimpse of her sneaking off. Set up on the grass were two folding chairs and a small table. The table was covered with a white cloth, beautifully set with silver cutlery and even candlesticks. A delicious meal was waiting for us. We had champagne and even chocolate-dipped strawberries."

It is strange hearing a story about Mum that I have never heard before. Listening to it now, I am filled with conflicting emotions. Almost as though it's about someone I don't know. The truth is I never did know the Lily Dad knew before they had me. A small part of me feels jealous at the thought of how many of these memories he must have stored in his head. At the same time, I realise how difficult it was for him to share that with me. I want him to know how much I appreciate him for it. Uncertain of how my voice will sound, I reach my hand in his direction until I find his arm, giving it a gentle squeeze.

"We're here!"

He announces, minutes later before turning off the engine. He comes round to open my door. Without removing my blindfold, he takes my hands, placing one on each of his shoulders, asking me to walk behind him. Very soon we stop. He unties and removes the cloth from my eyes. My vision is blurred from wearing the blindfold. Despite this, I can't miss the gigantic smiling face hovering high above us. We are at Luna Park.

When I was younger, this was my favourite place in the world. Whenever it was my birthday or any other special occasion, if I got to choose where we went, this is where we ended up. I have so many wonderful memories of being here with Mum, Dad and Rosie. Every memory I have of Luna Park is a positive one. I can't think of another place where this is the case.

If the smile on my face bears any relation to the one on Dad's, it must be huge. I take his hand. Together, we walk in through the enormous grinning mouth. The first ride we reach is one of my favourites. The Rotor is a cylindrical space. Park-goers stand with their backs against the walls. When the ride begins, the cylinder starts to spin, slowly at first, before gaining speed. Ultimately, the Rotor spins so fast that when the floor drops away, you find yourself stuck to the wall as if hanging in mid-air. Dad and I are holding hands, alternately laughing and screaming. When the ride ends, we are both giggling helplessly. We stagger out on wobbly legs like newborn calves. Still laughing, we make our way to a more sedate ride on the Ferris Wheel. The view of the harbour and city skyline, with the sunset as a backdrop, is breathtaking.

We go on as many rides as we can, twice on the dodgem cars, before eating dinner at the Lighthouse Café. After dinner, although we have just eaten, we buy some fairy floss for dessert. It was something Mum adored. Tonight, it just feels right. We pass the bag back and forth between us as we head back to the car for the drive home.

It is after nine-thirty when we walk in the door. Not wanting to take the shine off the evening neither of us comment on the answering machine's unblinking light. It was such a wonderful night. I am incredibly grateful to Dad for being so thoughtful. Nevertheless, I can't help thinking how amazing the evening would have been if Mum had been with us. I am in bed by ten thirty, lying on my side looking at the picture of the three of us. We all look so happy, so blissfully unaware of what the future holds for us. I pick up the picture, holding it to my chest. I cry myself to sleep.

# Chapter 30

Izzy, Toby and I walk together to the drama theatre. They chat about their group performance, which is about violence in the media. Once we arrive, Mr. Lennox asks us to get straight into our groups to carry on working. Dominic and Nick are already in the class, so I move to sit with them. It isn't long before Lauren arrives. We have decided to do our piece on cyber-bullying, with one narrator and three actors. We considered two story lines. I pushed for the one that would have allowed me to be the narrator, meaning I could definitely get away without touching anyone. Sadly, I was outvoted. The story the others opted for calls for two female actors. To start, Lauren, Dominic and I will all sit on chairs pretending to use computers. Lauren and I will face one way, Dominic the other, as he is to be the victim. Nick will read aloud the words while we pretend to type them.

The action then moves to school. One scene involves Lauren and I linking arms as we turn our backs on Dominic before walking off-stage. There is no way to avoid touching her. The sooner it is done the better. The three of us get up to practise. We move through the scenes until we reach the one I was hoping to avoid. Lauren links her arm through mine...

I find myself in a small, white room. A golden labrador lies on a narrow metal bed. Lauren's right arm is draped over the dog's middle, while his head is nestled in her left hand. His breathing is laboured. I can see cataracts in his rheumy eyes. Someone I can't see rests one hand supportively on my shoulder, while using the other to stroke my, that is Lauren's, back. A woman in a white coat has her back to us, as she does something unseen on the bench opposite.

Lauren is stroking the labrador. Each caress is imbued with feeling. I can feel tears streaming down her cheeks. She is muttering the dog's name and words of comfort to him. The vet turns slowly towards us, holding a syringe filled with a clear fluid. She looks at Lauren solemnly, before administering the shot. It doesn't take long for the life to seep out of him. Deefa seems to shudder slightly, before exhaling his last. The vet gently passes her hand over the dog's eyes, closing the lids. Lauren buries her face into Deefa's side as sobs rip through her...

Lauren's arm is no longer linked through mine, although I am standing statue-like, my arm still bent as if it were. Lauren is standing about three feet away from me. They are all staring at me anxiously.

"Are you alright, Juno?" Lauren asks.

"So sorry about that. I'm absolutely fine. Since... Well... Since my Mum... her accident... you know... Anyway, I just get these weird dizzy spells now and then. It looks really strange I know, but it's nothing to worry about, I promise. Let's practise that scene again."

My speech sounds garbled and comes out at warp speed, interspersed with bizarre-sounding, nervous chuckles. I am stumbling over myself in a desperate attempt to pacify them. Lauren's face still wears a look of concern. I ignore it, taking hold of her arm again, and manoeuvring her into our starting position. I sense Toby looking at me from across the room, checking to see if I am alright. I shoot him a reassuring smile. Lauren and I run through the scene again without incident.

My day finishes with double English. Mrs. Samuels asks us to consider the motif of ambition and self-improvement, with respect to Pip. As always when Mrs. Samuels is at the helm, the time flies. Once the bell has rung, I make my way out of class, finding Toby waiting in the hall. I wax lyrical about my English lesson as we walk out of the main building and down the stairs. Sophie is there waiting. The three of us make our way to the bus stop.

Astrid is still there when the two of us arrive home. After I have introduced her to Toby, she leads us through the lounge towards the kitchen. Walking through the living room, we are met by the delicious aroma of baking and we soon spy a batch of chocolate chip cookies, fresh out of the oven, lying temptingly on a baking tray. I put the kettle on. We are soon enjoying delicious, still-warm biscuits. Astrid disappears, using ironing as an excuse, leaving us alone. We both have a couple of pieces of homework due tomorrow, so decide to get them out of the way before Dad gets home.

When we are done, I show Toby around our home. It seems like forever since we have had a new visitor. Directly across the hall from the living area is my room. I decide to leave that till last. Instead, I lead him down the corridor, showing him the spare room, which used to be Rosie's, the bathroom and then the door to my parents' room. The phrase 'my parents' lingers menacingly in the air around us. I take a deep breath, clearing my throat before correcting myself and saying, "Dad's room". Toby gives my hand a squeeze. As we re-enter the hallway, Dad walks through the door.

"Hi, Juno, darling," he says, smiling as he walks towards us, his hand extended, "You must be Toby. Pleased to meet you."

"I'm very pleased to meet you too, sir," Toby says, pumping Dad's hand vigorously. He looks so nervous and sounds so formal that Dad actually laughs. It is a slightly awkward beginning, but Dad smoothes things over, asking Toby to call him Aaron. When Dad goes to change out of his suit, I take the opportunity to finish the house tour.

I lead Toby back to my room, opening the door. He walks to the centre of the room, and stands still. Very slowly, he starts looking around. I try to see the room as if for the first time, the way he is seeing it. For my fifteenth birthday, I was allowed to have it redecorated. I chose to have the ceiling white and the walls off-white, with one feature wall in bright purple. After a while, Toby walks over to my bedside table, picking up the photo of the three of us. He stares at it for a long while. Comfortingly, I find I don't need to look at it to know exactly what he is seeing.

We all meet in the living room. Dad starts asking Toby questions. I realise he is just trying to make conversation but it does sound a little like an interrogation. I have told Dad very little about Toby, which makes this question-and-answer session a little risky.

"Juno tells me your Dad is in the police force."

"Yes, that's right, he is an Inspector."

"So the move to Sydney was presumably due to your Dad's job?"

Toby hesitates here. If nothing else, the question confirms Dad's ignorance about Toby's situation, verifying that I have kept his secret. He glances briefly at me, before answering.

"Dad has been transferred here."

With this response, he has cleverly avoided lying, while at the same time seemingly answering Dad's question.

"Whereabouts in Melbourne were you living before?"

"I was born and raised in Richmond."

Thankfully, this answer helps steer the conversation to much safer waters. Dad is a huge fan of the Richmond football team. Before long, they are discussing the upcoming game against Hawthorn, and their chances of winning.

I leave them to it, going to the kitchen to see if Astrid needs any help. She tells me there is nothing to do. All the preparation has been done. Dinner will be ready in half an hour. With a flourish, she lifts the lid on a large pot. The smell that floats up at me is mouth-watering. Astrid says it is an old family recipe, something her grandmother called Chicken Surprise. Astrid prepares to leave. I promise to turn the stove off in twenty minutes, before serving the meal. As the phone begins to ring, I glance at the clock, which shows it is 6:30. I pounce on it. The sound of Rosie's voice, after a week without it, is like a tonic.

I say goodbye to Astrid, taking the receiver with me as I walk back through the living room. Dad and Toby are now discussing a particular player's return to form after injury. I signal to Dad that I will take the call in my room. As I pass through into the hall, I hear Dad explaining to Toby about Rosie's 6:30 calls.

"How are you feeling, Rosie?"

"I feel just fine, Juno, but more importantly, how are things with you?" Her words belie the weariness in her voice.

"Things are going pretty well actually."

I give her an abridged version of our session with Sylvia, as well as filling her in on the Luna Park outing. I am conscious of not taxing her energy at this point. Discussing my visions will have to wait until tomorrow night.

"What about that boy? Did you ever find out anything more about his memory?"

I can always count on Rosie to get straight to the heart of things.

"Yes, I did. You were right about everything. Both visions were related to the same memory. The reason I had the second one was because he had another emotional event, which created a new imprint."

"Mmm yes, I thought as much. Have you had any other unusual encounters?"

"The whole thing is unusual, but the answer is no, nothing stranger than normal."

Rosie is reassured that for now my Gift has not progressed at all. We sign off as we always do. I take the phone back into the living room, handing it to Dad, who speaks to Rosie from his seat on the couch. They don't talk long. His whole demeanour clearly portrays his relief at her return to us from that other place. Whenever she vanishes into that netherworld, there is always the very real fear she might never come back to us.

Astrid has left me with clear instructions and soon dinner is on the table. The three of us sit at the kitchen table while I serve up Astrid's Chicken Surprise with jasmine rice. The meal tastes as delectable as it smells. Conversation is kept to a minimum, peppered with noises of appreciation as we savour our meal. Astrid really went all out. There is even a pavlova for dessert which, with our bellies as full as they are, we can't possibly think of tackling yet. Together we clear the table, rinse the dishes, stacking them in the dishwasher, before moving back to the living area.

Dad brings out his backgammon set. I am relieved when Toby looks happy and eager to play. The three of us used to play often. We haven't played since the accident. The set is one Mum and I gave to Dad for his birthday a few years ago. Toby and I play first. I just beat him. Dad then beats me by a large margin, before Toby beats Dad. The atmosphere is light-hearted. Seeing the two of them together, it is hard to believe they only just met.

The competition has helped us work up an appetite for dessert. Dad plates up three heaped servings of pavlova, which we all manage to finish, before putting on the kettle, and making tea for us all. Dad asks us about school. We tell him which classes we share. I explain that Toby has been helping me with maths. After a brief pause in the conversation, Toby turns to my father.

"I wish I knew the right words to express my feelings, Aaron. What I'm trying to say is that I am so terribly sorry about what happened to Juno's mum."

If he had asked me beforehand whether this was a topic he should broach, I would have strongly warned him off. I am frantically trying to think of something to say. Before I can come up with anything, Dad replies.

"Thank you, Toby. I really mean that. She was a truly wonderful person. She was one of those people who absolutely loved life. She really managed to squeeze the most out of every day. She only had to walk into a room and, almost immediately, people noticed her. It wasn't her looks, although she really was a beautiful woman, it was more than that. People were naturally drawn to her. I only wish you had been able to meet her."

This is the first time since the funeral that I have heard Dad talk about Mum to someone other than me. It is difficult to hear. At the same time, it feels important. Another small step.

Once Toby senses Dad is talked out, he announces it is time to leave. He accepts Dad's offer of a lift home. The three of us leave together. Toby lives about five minutes away by car. At this time of night, there is very little traffic. When we arrive in his street, he tells us to stop at a single-storey house with a small front lawn. Before hopping out of the car, he thanks us both warmly for the evening. Dad lets him know he's welcome any time. Once we have driven off, Dad tells me that Toby seems like a fine young man, before adding with a smile, "I know your mum would have really liked him too."

# Chapter 31

My alarm goes off. I wake crying, even though I can't recall dreaming. It feels as though a huge, dark mass hovers over me. I imagined that discovering I was not responsible for Mum's accident would have eased my pain, might have made things easier to cope with. It seems the opposite is true. Whereas before, when I believed myself culpable, I felt I didn't deserve to mourn Mum, things have changed. Now, I have the right to fully feel the pain of her loss. It is as though an internal dam has burst. Finally, I am able to grieve. I need to get up. The energy required to drag my body out of bed just isn't available to me. The thought of going to school today is incredibly daunting.

Dad knocks on my door, before poking his head into the room. He takes one look at my face and stops, unsure what to do next.

"I'm ok, Dad, I really am. I'm just feeling a little sadder than usual today. I was thinking I might just have a day at home. Would that be alright with you?"

"Of course, darling, whatever you need. Maybe a long weekend will do you good."

As he says this, he walks across the room and sits on the edge of my bed. As I close my eyes he places his hand on my cheek...

I am once again sitting at the same desk as in my very first vision. I am looking at the same computer screen but instead of a spreadsheet, an email is open. The weather outside is overcast. The phone next to the framed photo of Mum and I rings. Once again, I watch as Dad's arm reaches to pick it up.

"Hello."

"Hello, Mr. Page, it's Oskar Hunter here."

"Hello, Oskar, have you got any news for me?"

"Well, actually, that's what I'm calling about. I have a client who's very interested in Juno's. I honestly didn't expect to find a potential buyer so soon. She had her first viewing on Monday, and has been back twice since. I have just received a call from her. She has made a very attractive offer, one I really think you ought to consider..."

I open my eyes. Dad gazes lovingly at me, his hands now safely in his lap. He doesn't seem to have noticed my disappearing act, for which I am grateful. It no doubt helped that I was lying down, with my eyes closed the entire time. I have barely given a thought to Juno's since Dad informed me of his decision to sell it. Suddenly, I want to see it more than anything.

"Dad, how long do you think it will take to sell Juno's?"

"Funny you should ask that, I had a call from the estate agent only yesterday. He called to tell me he has someone very interested. She's actually made a very decent offer, one I have decided to accept."

"Do you think it would be possible to take one last look at it before it sells?"

"Of course, I still have a set of keys. Hold on a minute, let me make a call and I'll be right back."

He leaves the room, closing the door behind him.

For the first time, it occurs to me that what is missing from my visions is the emotional component. I am able to watch events unfolding, but the only feelings present are my own. I have no way of knowing the mental state of the person who lived through the actual event in real time. In most cases, it is obvious what emotion would have been most prominent, but in some cases it is unclear. Obviously, the fact that the memory I just saw was charged enough for it to be seen by me means Dad had very strong feelings when he took that call. What they were, I can only guess at. Perhaps he was upset, but it's always possible that he was extremely relieved, happy even. Maybe we are in a hole financially, and selling Juno's will be a huge weight off his shoulders. I don't have any evidence at all to support this theory; however, based on the vision alone, it is a possibility. Perhaps, feeling the emotions that accompanied the memory is something that will come later. Maybe this is the type of progression Rosie warned me about.

Dad knocks, before walking back into my room, looking pleased with himself. "I have arranged to take the morning off work. How would you like to go and take a look at Juno's today?"

"Thanks, Dad, that would be perfect."

"Take your time getting ready. We'll have some breakfast, and then we'll go to Juno's."

"Sounds like a plan," I reply, sounding chirpier than I feel.

As we pull up outside Juno's, I am trying to recall the last time I was here, and am frustrated when I can't quite remember. Dad puts the key in the lock, and as soon as the door is open, we are hit by a fragrance that I will associate with this place forever. We walk through twinkling wind chimes, and green, blue and purple gossamer veils that Mum had hanging in the entrance. The veils were a physical representation of the division Mum wanted to create between the outside world and the haven that is Juno's.

I remember her telling me why she chose those particular veils. She explained that the colour green is symbolic of sanctuary. She wanted people walking into Juno's to be transported to a retreat, to be borne away from the stresses of modern life. Blue signifies peace and tranquility, exactly what Mum wanted Juno's to exude. Purple represents both imagination and spirituality, allowing people to get in touch with their deepest thoughts and feelings.

Once we are inside the shop, it is easy to imagine that Mum might walk in from out the back at any moment. I walk around, looking at all the things she chose to display. There are deliciously perfumed candles, silk pouches filled with potpourri, beautifully etched glass bottles containing bath oils, colourful vials of essential oils, handmade quilts, and dozens of different crystals. I run my fingers through the fringe around a beautiful lampshade, and sit on a quirky patchwork stool that Mum adored. It is impossible to be here and not feel Mum's presence. I am certain that this should be a comforting feeling, but it isn't. Instead, it unsettles me, and makes her absence all the more real.

I feel like I am on the precipice of a huge canyon and only by sheer force of will can I stop from plummeting into the abyss.

Suddenly, I have an overwhelming urge to leave. I jump up, turning for the door and, in my haste, catch my foot on the corner of the stool and wind up in a heap on the floor. I am not hurt, at least not physically, but I am crying anyway.

"Juno, darling, did you hurt yourself?"

All I can do in reply is shake my head, tears coursing down my face. Soon I am weeping so loudly that even I find it hard to hear. Dad is kneeling next to me. He works his right arm underneath my shoulders and his left underneath my knees, before scooping me up in his arms. I can't remember the last time he held me like this, but I haven't forgotten what to do. I wrap my arms round his neck and stay like that until my sobbing dwindles.

When he gently places me back on my feet, I turn, taking one last look at the place my mother loved as much as our home, before walking out the door.

# Chapter 32

The surgery waiting room is empty when Sue takes her break. I am beginning to think that I may be lucky enough to get away without having to touch anyone today, when the door to the waiting room opens. I instantly recognise the man who enters as the same man who arrived while I was leaving last week. I remember thinking how familiar he looked at the time, and how seeing him made me so uncomfortable. Both those feelings return now, even more intensely than before. Where have I seen him before? Checking in the appointment book, I find that his name is Zachary Sharp, but this doesn't help me at all.

I wonder if it is just from seeing him here some time ago, but the memory feels more recent. It's not as though I meet many men other than the teachers at school. I have hardly been anywhere other than school and Greenfields since I came out of hospital. Suddenly, I remember exactly where I have seen him. He was sprawled on a couch, watching a cricket game, before slamming his fist into the red-headed Nurse Rachel's arm.

The memory makes me shudder, and the thought that I will have to touch him is so repulsive that I actually begin to feel nauseous. I wait another few minutes, desperately hoping that Sue will return. When I finally accept that I have no choice but to attend to him, I move to the waiting room door. Sliding it open I say, "Please follow me, Mr. Sharp", all the while avoiding eye contact.

As he was only here last week, weighing him is unnecessary. My mouth is dry and when I ask him to sit, my voice sounds shaky. Taking a deep breath, I affix the blood pressure cuff to his arm. Once it is inflated, I sit down before gingerly placing my fingers on his pulse…

I am immediately in a darkened bedroom, where a naked woman is lying face down on a bed. Her hands and feet are bound to the four corners of the bed-posts and there is something tied at the back of her head. She is barely moving, but I can hear her whimpering through the gag. Her red hair is tied back but I can see a small tattoo at the base of her neck in the shape of a V…

My nausea has worsened so much so that I am dizzy and my hands have become clammy. The monster sitting opposite me actually looks concerned as suddenly I jump out of my seat, and run to the sink in the corner of the room. My breakfast is soon out of me, but the horrible feeling is still with me. I run water until the sink is clean, and am rinsing out my mouth when Sue returns.

"Hangover, huh?" smirks the sorry excuse for a man, just as Sue walks into the room.

"Juno, are you ok? Are you ill?"

"I feel awful, it must have been something I ate. I'm really sorry, Sue, but is it ok if I leave now?"

"Of course, you poor thing. Do you need me to call you a cab?"

"Thank you, but no. I think the fresh air will do me good."

I can't get out of the place quick enough. In no time at all, I have grabbed my things and am riding the elevator the five floors down to the street.

Toby isn't due for a while, so I walk towards the bus stop. I buy a juice on the way, both to increase my sugar levels and to improve the taste in my mouth. I still feel vaguely nauseous, and am a little shaky. What do I do now? I have no idea *when* he tied up that poor nurse or how long she was left like that. Maybe she's still tied up even now. Do I go to the police? What would I tell them? These questions chase each other round and round my head until Toby arrives. He sees in an instant that I'm distressed.

"Juno, you really don't look well. Is everything alright?"

"Toby, I have to talk to you. I touched a patient, and saw something horrible, and now I don't know what to do."

We decide to head to the nearest park where we can talk privately. His arm is slung protectively around my shoulders as we walk, and the realisation that I don't have to deal with this alone helps to calm me down.

The only other people in the park are a woman and her young daughter, but they are over at the playground equipment, the mother pushing her daughter on a swing. We find a patch of grass, and sit with the late afternoon sun on our backs.

"Tell me what you saw."

"Firstly, I need to tell you that back when all this started, the second vision I had was with a nurse in the hospital."

I describe Nurse Rachel's memory before going on.

"Last Saturday, when I was leaving the surgery, the man who hit Rachel was walking into the surgery while I was walking out. He looked familiar, and just walking past him gave me the creeps, but I didn't place him - until I saw him again today. I had to take his blood pressure, and when I touched him, I saw his girlfriend naked and tied face down to a bed. Her wrists and ankles were tied to the corners of the bed, and she was gagged!"

I am expecting his face to mirror the emotions I am still dealing with, having witnessed the scene. Instead, he calmly asks me if I have considered the possibility that the nurse was a willing participant rather than being tied up against her will.

This had not occurred to me at all, and as I consider it, I realise that it may well be the case.

"Well, no, but I definitely heard her groaning."

"Yes, but that alone isn't enough to prove for certain that he has done anything wrong."

We talk it over a while, and by the time we are ready to go home, I am much calmer, and convinced that I had naively jumped to conclusions. After all, nobody is forcing Nurse Rachel to remain in a relationship with Zachary Sharp. If she wants to, all she has to do is leave. Perhaps both the scenes I saw that had upset me so much were just part and parcel of their normal interactions. I readily accept that I lead a sheltered life, and have been exposed to very little. Who knows what goes on in other people's lives?

When I get home, Dad tells me Rosie called and she sends her love. I feel a flash of guilt, which he immediately douses by saying, "She was over the moon when I told her you were out with Toby, and she can't wait to see you tomorrow." Despite what Toby told me, I can't totally rid myself of the feeling that the nurse is in trouble. I toss and turn for what seems like hours, before eventually drifting off to sleep.

# Chapter 33

The kitchen calendar shows it is May sixteenth. Exactly one month since Mum died. Although I don't mention it, clearly Dad is as aware as I am. Breakfast is a sombre affair. The car ride is equally quiet, but the radio is on. I find my eyes welling with tears as a song that reminds me of Mum is played. I keep my head turned to look out the window until it is over.

The sky is a cornflower blue, and there is a gentle breeze blowing as we make our way to Greenfields' main door. Rosie is there, beautifully groomed, and sitting in a high-backed chair smiling happily at us. She asks us to go straight into the garden, and as she stands she bends to reach down for a bag I had not initially noticed. I look at her questioningly as I take the bag from her, but she just smiles benignly, giving nothing away. She takes Dad's arm, and together the three of us walk down the main steps into the garden.

Once we are seated at one of the wooden benches dotted around the garden, Rosie takes my hand and one of Dad's in each of hers.

It appears Rosie has something to say, so we wait quietly until she is ready.

"I understand what a difficult day this is for all of us, and how many more difficult days there are to come."

Dad and I share a look. We should have known better than to try and hide anything from her.

"The thing is Lily would so hate to see either of you sad. You know what she was like. Even as a child, if ever I got teary over a movie or something I read, she would come right up to me, as close as she could, and look in my eyes trying to spot tears. If she saw or even imagined she saw the slightest hint of a tear, she would wipe it away, begging me not to cry."

Rosie asks me to pass her the bag, and once she has it in her lap, she reaches into it. She pulls out a leather-bound photo album, which she places in her lap.

"I am going to show you this memory book I started to make when Lily was born. I've added to it slowly over the years."

On the inside cover of the album, a piece of paper has been taped and folded shut. Rosie unfolds it to reveal a family tree, dating back to Rosie's great-grandparents. The names and dates are in Rosie's unmistakeable hand, all upward sloping lines and even spacing. My eyes are immediately drawn to Mum's name, which is towards the bottom of the page, a box neatly ruled around it. I notice with a start that Rosie has recently entered the date of her death, so that beneath her name it reads 04/12/1968 - 16/04/2010. A horizontal line next to her name links her to Aaron Page; from the centre of that, a vertical line drops and there, at the very bottom, is my name and date of birth, 25/10/1994.

Rosie folds the family tree away, and turns to the first page. There is a small, colour photograph, bordered in white. In it, Rosie is wearing a white top and shorts, and is standing on the balcony of a pale brick building, smiling hugely as she squints into the sun. In her arms, wrapped in a pink crocheted blanket, is a baby whose features are indecipherable. Stuck on the page next to it is a photocopy of Lily's birth certificate.

There is a page depicting a huge open mouth, showing each upper and lower tooth. Next to each tooth are two dates, all written at varying times. Rosie explains that the first date is when she noticed the tooth's appearance in Mum's mouth, and the second date is when the tooth fell out. As Rosie slowly turns the pages, we watch Lily grow from a baby to a round-faced, fair-haired toddler, standing in her cot, wearing an all-in-one, and looking straight at the camera.

"Every morning she would stand up and call out 'Mamma', 'Dadda' until one of us appeared."

Soon, she is a little girl with long, honey- blonde pigtails, in tights, a polo-necked jumper and navy skirt, standing next to a young and beautiful Rosie, wearing a matching jumper and skirt, but minus the pigtails.

"She so loved it when we wore the same outfit."

On another page, she is a wistful-looking girl of around ten, in a gypsy skirt and peasant top, her hair loose and her feet bare. Next, she is a teenager, in hot-pink Lycra pants, a silver top and roller skates on her feet, beaming at the camera as she goes off to a disco party. Rosie has added a small footnote to each picture.

After several pages, Dad makes his first appearance on the night of Mum's school formal. He is wearing a tuxedo and his arms are around Lily, who is wearing a beautiful, black taffeta dress and huge silver earrings. Looking at photos of my parents, so young and vibrant, so clearly in love with each other, is wonderful and dreadful in equal measure. I risk a sidelong look at Dad, and can see he is suffering. A few pages later is a wedding photo that I have not seen before. Mum is standing, looking jubilant, graceful and elegant in her sheath wedding dress. Dad stands behind her, looking dapper, wearing a joyful expression, his arms loosely draped around her slender waist.

Rosie keeps turning the pages, adding observations here and there. Before long, there are photos of the three of us, and just like time-lapse photography, I watch myself grow from a tiny swaddled new-born through toddlerhood, girlhood and adolescence. The last picture is an exact copy of the one I now have by my bed.

"Lily gave that one to me. Such a gorgeous photo of you all."

Once she has closed the book, she turns to me and, holding it in both hands, passes it to me.

"This is for you now, Juno. I know you will cherish it as much as I always have."

"But Rosie," I protest, "You should keep it until…"

The rest of the sentence dies in my mouth and I could kick myself.

"Juno, it was always meant for you. Now that Lily is gone, I am giving it to you a little earlier, that's all."

She has one of her hands covering one of mine, and is administering a small amount of pressure as she says this. It is her way of telling me that she has made up her mind, and to argue would be wasted effort.

I put the book back into its bag, and Rosie announces that she needs to freshen up before lunch.

"Juno, darling, would you mind walking with me back to my room?"

Marvelling at Rosie's intuitiveness, I readily agree. She clearly senses that Dad needs some time to gather himself, after having all those memories paraded before him.

Dad smiles at me sadly as Rosie takes my arm, and we slowly begin walking towards the entrance. She asks how my night was, giving my arm a playful tug as she does. I tell her a bit about Toby, before diving headlong into my newest dilemma. First, I remind her about my vision of Nurse Rachel's memory, and then tell her about recognising her boyfriend yesterday. I recount the experience I had with him in the surgery. I also explain my initial fear that the nurse is in real danger, and then share Toby's theory with her.

"Maybe Toby's right, but there's still a nagging doubt in my mind. Even before I remembered where I had seen him, something about him made me really uneasy. The thing is, Rosie, when I have a vision I get to see the memory as clearly as if I were actually there, but what's missing is the feeling. I have no idea what the person *felt* when the event took place. If I could have tapped into the emotional state of that man as he stood looking at her tied up like that, I might know one way or the other. But really, thinking about it, even if I was absolutely sure she was in danger, what could I do?"

"Hmm, yes, Juno, that's a lot to take on board. My advice would always be to trust your gut with this sort of thing. You were the one who had the vision, and there's always the possibility that some small detail, something you can't even recall now, something you saw or heard while you were reliving the memory, gave you the impression she was in trouble."

I think about that possibility, but I am fairly certain that I didn't see or hear anything other than exactly what I reported to Toby yesterday, and again to Rosie just now. Perhaps Toby is right, and it was just my reaction at seeing her tied up that made me instantly assume she was there against her will.

As we arrive at Rosie's room, she interrupts my thoughts. "But as you say, Juno, it's the question of what to do with the information that proves difficult to answer." Rosie seems preoccupied with this thought. "Juno, there's something else I wanted to talk to you about."

"Sure, what is it?"

"Well there's one more relative of mine that had the Gift, one I haven't mentioned yet."

I nod for her to go on, although something makes me think I may not want to hear it. Just as Rosie goes to speak again, Dad joins us.

"Ready for lunch, ladies?"

If he notices the looks that pass between Rosie and myself, he doesn't acknowledge it.

Together, the three of us walk to the crowded dining room. I am pleased to see Eric looking remarkably healthy and robust, sitting in between his son Bruce and daughter-in-law Claire. We sit opposite them, Dad in between Rosie and I, so there is no opportunity to continue our talk. After lunch, Rosie walks us back to the main entrance, and as soon as Dad goes ahead to get the car, Rosie continues where she left off.

"Juno, what I have to tell you will take more time than we have now. I would really prefer to be able to have the conversation face-to-face, but things don't seem to have worked out that way."

My full attention is on Rosie so I jump slightly when Dad gives the horn a small toot, letting me know he is here and ready to go. As I lean in to kiss Rosie, she whispers in my ear,

"I'll call tonight, and we'll have a good chat then."

We are quiet on the trip home, both lost in our own thoughts. I am eager to look at the family tree again, but don't want to risk upsetting Dad by taking the book out here. Instead I listen to the radio, and look at the passing scenery.

Once I am back in my room, I take out the album and open the family tree again. I run my fingers over the names of my ancestors: Mary, my great-great grandmother, b.19/10/1894- d.9/7/1968. Ava, Mary's daughter, and mother of Rosie, b.06/01/1917 - d.19/05/1973. My great aunt Frances, b.24/09/1935 - d.15/11/1961 and next to her, Rosie b.04/04/1937 - _____. Alongside Rosie is my grandfather Norman, b.10/07/1930- d.31/12/1988. Something next to Frances' name catches my eye. It is a small asterisk. I run my eyes slowly over the page, and find the mark repeated beside Mary and Ruby's names and at the bottom of the page by mine. It doesn't take a rocket scientist to work out what the mark means. Just as I am about to fold the family tree shut, I notice another asterisk. I am stunned to see the mark by my mother's name.

My mind goes blank as this information gradually filters in, and then all of a sudden, my brain is besieged by questions. What was her Gift? Why didn't she tell me about it? Did Dad know? Why hasn't

Rosie told me about it? Immediately, I understand that this is what Rosie wants to talk to me about.

The rest of the afternoon seems to crawl by at a snail's pace. I do homework to pass the time, but it seems endless. While part of me is frightened to hear what Rosie has to say, by the time 6:30 comes and goes, the suspense is eating me up. As the hands of the clock move past 7:00, I experience a sinking feeling. Is it possible that she has forgotten? Or perhaps her mental state has deteriorated since we were with her? When the phone rings at seven fifteen, I jump up to get it.

"It's probably Toby," I say, as I answer the call. I am gratified to hear Rosie's voice. As Rosie never normally calls after a visit, I don't want to alarm Dad by letting on that it's her. I don't want to tell him an outright lie, so I say nothing. Instead, as I pass him on the way to my room, I give him a look that might be read as confirmation that it is Toby on the phone.

"Hi, Rosie," I whisper, although it is an unnecessary precaution as my bedroom door is shut and Dad has the television on.

"Hi, Juno, I hope you weren't worried. I don't normally call on Sundays, and I thought if I called at my usual time, your Dad might be a bit suspicious."

Trust Rosie to think of everything. "No Rosie, I wasn't worried." This is not really a lie, more of a fib.

"Oh, good. Now, Juno, as I said earlier, ideally we would be having this chat face-to-face, but something tells me I shouldn't wait too long, so there we have it."

Rosie hesitates, and it is clear she is not finding this easy, so I try to be as patient as possible. She takes an audibly deep breath, before beginning to speak.

"Your Mum and I were very close, Juno, as you know, and very rarely did we disagree about anything, but unfortunately, this is one of those things. Have you had a close look at the family tree?"

"Yes."

"And did you notice anything in particular?"

"Yes."

"I thought you might. Well, let me tell it from the beginning. When Lily was four years of age, she fell off a pony, and suffered quite a severe head injury. She was hospitalised, and while she was still there, she developed bacterial meningitis. She was ill for a couple of months and sadly, not long after she came home, my mother became unwell. My mother was a big part of our lives, often looking after Lily when she got home from pre-school while I worked, but we all did our best to keep her illness from Lily. Early in 1973, the doctors explained that my mother had bowel cancer, and that it was too far gone to be treated. Lily and I visited her regularly, but only when she was feeling well enough. Otherwise, I visited when Lily was in pre-school.

"Near the end, she was so sick and weak that I told Lily her grandmother had gone away on a long holiday. I couldn't bear for her to remember my mother that way. We moved her into a hospice at the end of April as it was getting harder and harder for us to take proper care of her. On the morning of

May nineteen, I received a call from the hospice, informing me that Ava had passed away. I don't need to tell you how that made me feel, and despite the best of intentions Lily noticed my mood immediately.

"I'll never forget it, Juno. She came into the kitchen where I was sitting, and said to me,

'It's ok, Mum. Grandma is better now. She won't be hurting anymore.'

"I was so incredibly astonished by what she said that for whole minutes I couldn't speak, but Lily went about eating her breakfast, as if nothing extraordinary had happened. When I had regained my composure, I sat at the table opposite her and asked her how she knew Grandma was gone. She simply replied, 'I just did.' She was a very intuitive child, so I wasn't absolutely certain what it meant, but I had a fairly good idea in that moment, that my little girl had the Gift.

"I was almost able to forget about it, until she was six. One Friday after school, out of the blue, she mentioned she had said goodbye to her friend Donna, because she wouldn't be seeing her again for a very long time. When I asked her where Donna was going, she said 'Heaven', without skipping a beat. It is so clear in my memory, Juno, as though it happened yesterday. I was standing at the sink, peeling potatoes for Friday night dinner. When she said the word 'Heaven', it was like someone had poured a bucket of iced water over me. My whole body broke out in goosebumps, and a huge shudder ran through me. Lily was at the kitchen table colouring and, thankfully, had her back to me. Something made me nervous to look at her, lest she detect my unease, so without turning to face her, I asked why she thought a perfectly healthy six year old was going to heaven. All she said was, 'It's her time.' I remember how my heart sank when she said this, but I was careful to keep my anxieties to myself. After she went to bed, I agonised over what to do, much like you are doing now. Donna's mother Anna was a woman I knew, but she was not a particularly close friend. I wanted to warn her, but what on earth was I going to say? I couldn't talk to your grandfather about it. Sadly, Frances had passed away before I met Norman, as had my Great-Aunt Ruby, so he never witnessed their gifts in action. He thought the tales about them were just that, tales. He was there when my grandmother Mary predicted that Lily would be a girl, but later laughed that with a fifty per cent chance of being right, it wasn't all that impressive.

"In the end, I did nothing, and it's something I have never been able to forgive myself for. While Lily was at school on the Monday, I received a phone call from one of the other school mothers. She had called to tell me that Donna had drowned in a neighbour's pool on the Saturday, and although she was still alive when the ambulance arrived at the hospital, she died later that same evening. Clearly, I needed no more proof of your mother's Gift. My biggest concern now was trying to keep her from letting anybody else know about it.

"The fact that she was so young made it a little easier. The likelihood of her encountering people old enough to be close to death was fairly small. I reasoned that she probably had no idea that she was different, assuming everybody capable of the same foresight, so that helped too. It wasn't until she was twelve, when I was sure she could handle the information, that I told her that being able to tell when someone was going to die was not something that everybody could do. I remember how incredulous she was, initially learning that.

"When she was young, she was only able to tell people were going to pass, close to, or just before it happened. As she got older, her ability became more acute, and soon she was able, just by touching someone, to know exactly when they would die. Like you, she felt the Gift was a great burden, something to be denied whenever possible. She made me vow that I would never divulge her secret to anybody. I was surprised when she told me that she was never going to tell Aaron, but I didn't argue with her, as the decision was hers to make, and nothing to do with me.

"It wasn't until she had you that we began to disagree. I felt that being a girl it was something that you needed to be aware of at some point, but your mother was absolutely adamant that you never be told. I waited, sure that when you were a bit older she would feel differently, but she never did. When you turned thirteen, I begged her to tell you about the Gift in general, about Mary, Ruby and Frances, and to leave herself out of the story altogether, but she wouldn't hear of it. She felt that since you didn't have the Gift, there was no need to concern you with any knowledge of it. I tried reasoning with her. My concern was that you might one day give birth to a daughter, who developed the Gift. Surely it made sense that you have some knowledge of it, just in case? I didn't push too hard though as I always assumed that were you to have a daughter, Lily would be around, and would almost definitely change her mind then."

We both fall silent. Of course, I too always imagined that my mother would be by my side when I had a baby. The thought of all the years ahead of us, without her in our lives, is an oppressive weight. We are both alone with our thoughts for a while before Rosie resumes speaking.

"As soon as I became aware that you had the Gift, I knew I had to tell you about the family history, but the promise I made to

Lily stopped me from telling you about her. A couple of days ago, I received a visit from Sophie's mum Annie. She came especially because, about six weeks before her accident, Lily entrusted her with a sealed envelope to be given to me should anything happen to her while I was still alive. If you turn to the very last page of the book I gave you today, you will find it. Juno, my darling, I am tired after talking so much. I love you."

"I love you more." My voice is almost inaudible, my mind barely able to process all I have heard.

"Impossible," says Rosie before ending the call.

My poor mother. Even trying to imagine what it might be like to know when someone is going to die, years before they actually do, is terrifying. It seems as far as the Gift goes that I have gotten off relatively easy. I return the phone to the kitchen, telling Dad I am going to have an early night. I take my time getting ready for bed, feeling a strange mixture of curiosity and apprehension. I bring Rosie's memory book into bed with me, tentatively opening it to the last page. The envelope is a plain white one, with *Mum* written on it in my mother's familiar hand. Rosie has resealed the envelope, and I prise it open again very carefully. Nervously, I unfold the letter and read it.

*5th March, 2010*

*Dear Mum,*

*If you're reading this, it is because, despite my best efforts, I have failed to alter my destiny.*

*I have known for as long as I can remember that I am due to die on April 16th of this year. In an attempt to rewrite my fate, I have had comprehensive medical examinations bi-annually. My last one was four months ago, and I was given a clean bill of health, so I have to assume that I will be involved in an accident of some kind.*

*I know you will be angry that I didn't come to you with this information, but please try and understand that it was something I never wanted to burden you with.*

*I have thought about staying home that day to minimise my chances of being involved in an accident but the real fear that in doing so I may somehow endanger either Aaron or Juno means that I will not.*

*My plan is to alter my normal routine in such a way as to increase my chances of surviving while also limiting the possibility of putting others at risk. I am only telling you this in case the circumstances of my death cause confusion. I need you to know that I did everything I could to stay alive.*

*Please know how much I love, admire and respect you. I could not have wished for a better mother, or friend.*

*Now that I am gone, I ask that you please share everything with Juno. Even though she doesn't have the Gift, it is important that she is aware of the situation, in case, as you yourself pointed out, she should ever give birth to a daughter.*

*Please understand my reason for waiting until after I am gone before allowing Juno to know. At least this way, all the knowledge I have dies with me.*

*Saying thank you seems inadequate, as words alone are incapable of allowing me to properly express my gratitude for the love you showered me with all my life.*

*I will love you always and forever.*
*Lily*

I re-fold the letter, put it in its envelope, and slip it back into the book, which I then place into my bedside table drawer. The sadness is paralysing. Surrendering to the pain, I cry myself to sleep.

# Chapter 34

A thick, soupy fog surrounds me, and although I can't see anything, I am not afraid to walk forward. I know somebody is ahead of me, somebody I need to find, somebody who is looking for me. As if guided by something unseen, I travel forwards, moving deftly through the miasma. Slowly, the haze seems to thin out, and finally clears altogether. I find myself walking across a small brook, stepping over a path of stones washed smooth by water. Trees as tall as buildings form a wall ahead of me. I look for a way through and, finding none, turn back to the rivulet, only to find it is now a raging river that cannot possibly be crossed. I am unafraid as I cast around in search of something to help me, and spot a small boat leaning against a rock. I easily pull it to the water, and hop in. The water carries me swiftly along in its flow for a while and then, quite suddenly, the boat comes to a stop, right alongside the riverbank. Stepping onto the bank, I see flowers everywhere, and an enormous, solitary tree. Its boughs stretch far and wide, casting a perfectly, circular shadow on the grass below. Someone is sitting beneath the tree, the one I have been searching for.

I move towards the tree, to where I belong, and sit on the soft cool grass, facing my father.

When Sophie and I arrive at school, there is an atmosphere of palpable tension. In a matter of minutes, Georgie and Izzy find us, and we learn the cause. Mr. Fitzgerald has called a 'Special Whole School Assembly'. Regular assemblies for the whole school occur only on the first day of each term. Thinking back, the last 'Special Assembly' I can remember was years ago, when my teacher Mrs. Dunn's husband had passed away. I am lost in thought, but soon become aware that people are surreptitiously looking at me. I am initially bewildered, but then it hits me. Of course... the last time they remember this happening was merely weeks ago, when they were called together to hear about Mum. Sophie has her arm linked through mine protectively, as though to ward off any unwanted attention.

Toby walks up to join us, and immediately Georgie fills him in, breathlessly running her words together, as only Georgie can.

"We just heard that Mr. Fitzgerald has called a 'Special Whole School Assembly', which almost never happens, and it's never good news either, it's always to tell us something *really* bad has happened. The last one was when Lily, you know, Juno's mum... Well you know."

At this she turns to me and adds "Sorry, Juno," as she dramatically throws her arms around me, pulling me to her. Sophie, Toby and Izzy all shoot me empathetic looks. Despite Georgie's theatricality, I don't doubt for a moment that her love for Lily was sincere.

The assembly has been called for 8:40, which is when first period usually starts. At least we won't be in suspense for too long. Students gather together in huddles, and speculation is rife. Toby suddenly remembers he needs to collect something from his locker, and asks if I will go with him. We make a plan to meet the others outside the hall, just before the assembly is due to start. Toby takes hold of my hand as we walk up the steps into the main building. Once we are in the hall, he stops walking and turns to me.

"I think I know what this assembly is about."

"Really? How come?"

"Dad called last night to let me know that he wouldn't be home until very late, if at all, which only happens when they are working on something really big. Anyway, he explained that a sixteen-year-old girl had been reported missing. I've never heard of her, which isn't surprising, but she's a student at *this* school."

"Oh, that's awful! If she's sixteen, she must be in our year. Do you know who it is?"

"Her name's Piper somebody or other, I don't remember her surname."

Suddenly I am dizzy, and can hear nothing but white noise. Toby has his hands on my shoulders, and is saying something but I can't hear a word. He lets go of me, but when I nearly collapse, he stops my fall and leads me into the nearest classroom, helping me to sit. I put my head between my knees, and wait until the whooshing in my ears and the giddiness disappear. When I am feeling well enough to sit up, Toby hands me my water bottle that he has dug out of my bag. Once I have regained my composure, I apologise, explaining to Toby that the news about Piper has upset me terribly.

"I was worried you were having another one of your visions. I wanted to make it stop and that's why I let go of you. When you started to fall, I realised something else was going on."

"It was just shock, I think I nearly fainted."

"So, you know her?"

"Yes, well... no, not really. I actually know very little about her. She only started at Edgecliff High at the beginning of this school year. She's in my history class, that's all, and we often sit next to each other. It's just such a shock. What did your father tell you?"

"Only that she lives with an aunt, who is her legal guardian. The last time she saw her was after school on Friday. Apparently, Piper went out that night, but her aunt has no idea where. The aunt worked all day Saturday, and didn't get home till quite late, so it wasn't until Sunday that she finally realised Piper was missing. She has no idea whether Piper ever made it home on Friday night, or if she has been missing since then."

As we leave the classroom, I am reminded about the memory of Piper's that I saw only a week ago.

As we walk back into the corridor, teachers and students alike are filing out of the building. We follow them, and join everybody else going into the hall. The others are all outside the entrance waiting for us, and step into line as we walk past. Mr. Fitzgerald is already standing on the stage in conversation with two men and a woman, none of whom I have ever seen before. As we are taking our seats, Toby whispers in my ear. "The man to the right of Mr. Fitzgerald is my dad."

Before I have a chance to respond, Mr. Fitzgerald is addressing us.

"Settle down, everyone. This is important, so I need you all to be listening carefully. Unfortunately, I have called you all here to let you know that a member of our student body has been reported missing."

A collective gasp goes up around the room. He allows this shocking information to sink in for a while, before calling for quiet, and continuing,

"A Year Ten student, Piper Reid, went out on Friday night."

At the mention of Piper's name, the noise in the hall escalates. The girls are all looking at each other, and I watch as they register the news. Sophie's mouth hangs open, and as our eyes meet, she quickly registers that my face is not reflecting the same emotions as hers. I am relieved to have been prepared, and not to be hearing the news for the first time. Mr. Fitzgerald calls for silence again, before announcing,

"Her guardian does not know who she went out with, or where she was going or, in fact, if she ever made it home that night."

He pauses here and given the amount of people in the room, the quiet is remarkable. Finally, he says, "Piper hasn't been seen since."

He hesitates again, before gesturing to the people behind him and saying, "Inspector Moxham would like to have a few words with you."

Toby's father steps forward to speak, and I watch as understanding dawns on Sophie's face. Looking at Toby's dad, the resemblance is clear: they have the same oval face, high forehead and almond-shaped eyes.

"Hello, everyone. I am very sorry to be here under these circumstances. In cases like these, time is of the essence, so I will keep it as brief as I can. The bottom line is we need your help. We have very little to go on, and without more information, we will waste precious time. Detectives Kalifeh and Parsons will be here in the gymnasium all day."

As he says this, he indicates the man and woman, standing to his left.

"We need you to come and see them, if you have *any* information at all about Piper. I stress the word any, because cases like these are often solved with the *smallest* details. If any of you were with her on Friday night, spoke to her, or even saw her across the room, we want you to come and tell us. Even if you are certain that something you know *isn't* important. Even if you believe the piece of information you have could have *nothing* at all to do with her disappearance, we need to know it. I stress again: *no* detail is too small. Thank you, all. Let's hope that with your help we can quickly locate Piper, and have her safely back home."

Mr. Fitzgerald then reiterates the importance of us holding nothing back, before dismissing us. Once we have left the hall, Sophie draws alongside me. She doesn't have to say anything, I know what she is thinking. I tell her I will go to see them during break, to which she nods approvingly.

When I enter the gymnasium, the two detectives are seated behind one large desk in the centre of the room. They seem overly pleased to see me, and I wonder if anyone else has come to volunteer information. The female detective introduces herself as Detective Parsons, and asks me a few personal details, which she records on a sheet of paper, before asking me to tell her what I know.

"This may not be at all helpful, but you wanted to know everything, so I thought I should let you know what I saw."

She nods eagerly, urging me to go on.

236

"Well, two weeks ago, I was out on Saturday night, and I saw Piper going into The Sheaf Hotel."

"Was she with someone?"

"When I saw her, I was standing on the other side of the road, walking in the opposite direction, but from what I can recall seeing, she appeared to be alone."

"What time was that?"

"Around eight-thirty."

"Is there anything else you think we should know?"

"Well, it's nothing really, just that she was very dressed up. Well, I mean she looked very different."

"She was out of uniform, right?"

"Yes, but it was more than that."

"I'm not sure I understand what you are saying."

"What I mean is… the girls at school either wear their uniform the regular way, or they change it."

"How do you mean?"

"They shorten the skirt, wear blouses that are a little small, that sort of thing."

"What about Piper?"

"That's the thing… her skirt is far longer than almost anyone's. Her blouse is a little too large, shapeless even. She always wears her hair in the same style, plaited and then tied up in a bun."

"But when you saw her out?"

"It was the absolute opposite. She had on a tight, short, denim skirt, a strapless top, high heels and her hair was loose. She looked nothing like the Piper that comes to school."

"And you're absolutely certain it was her?"

"Absolutely."

Just as I am about to get up to leave, I remember something,

"There's one more thing. I'm not one hundred per cent certain about this, but I am pretty sure that Piper has a tattoo on the back of her neck."

An unmistakable look passes between the two detectives, and I realise that this is not news to them. This explains why they don't press me for details regarding the tattoo.

"Thank you, Juno, we'll be in touch if we have any further questions. Please don't hesitate to contact us if anything else comes to mind."

The rest of the day is a bit of a blur. The teachers seem to be as disturbed by Piper's disappearance as the students. In English, Mrs. Samuels spends the whole double period just reading to us; even Mr. Hardy had little to say, choosing to have us watch a movie on World War II. Despite the fact that we learnt nothing all day, I am totally exhausted by the end of it.

On the bus ride home, Sophie asks me about my interview with the detectives.

"I told them what I told you - that I saw her out that Saturday night, that she was going into The Sheaf, and I described what she was wearing."

"Do you think it helped at all?"

"I have no idea, but I guess it might. Perhaps she is a regular at The Sheaf. Maybe that's where she was on Friday night. Maybe some of the staff will recognise her photo, and remember who she was with. Maybe it won't help at all, but I feel better for having told them."

"I wonder if anyone else went to see them. Did you see anyone else coming or going into the gym?"

"Not while I was there."

"I wonder where she could be? I really hope nothing's happened to her. I mean, maybe she just ran away? Maybe she met some guy, and they left together?"

"Sophie, there's something I haven't told you. It may have nothing to do with anything, but I just need another point of view, someone else to listen to it and give me their opinion."

"Sure, Juno, what is it?"

"Exactly a week ago, I sat next to Piper in history. I guess I've always been curious about her, but after I saw her out that weekend, I was even more so. I didn't really plan it beforehand, but sitting there listening to Mr. Hardy waffling on, I suddenly decided to try and touch her to see if I would have a vision. I moved my arm until it touched hers, and it worked! I mean I saw something."

"What did you see?" Sophie is perched on the edge of her seat, twisted to face me, her eyes wide in anticipation.

"I saw her sitting in a courtroom. There was a woman standing in front of me. I couldn't see her face as she had her back to me, but she was tall and slim like Piper, and also had red hair. I'm about as sure as I can be that it was her mother. Anyway, this woman was standing before the judge, and the judge was about to sentence her, and then suddenly it was over."

"Did it end because that was all there was, or was it because you stopped touching her?"

"I'm not absolutely certain, but I assume it was because we stopped touching. When it was over, she was sitting back in her chair with her arms folded."

"So you think her mum's in jail?"

"Yes, exactly."

"Maybe it has something to do with why she moved here. I wonder who she lives with now?"

"The guardian Mr. Fitzgerald mentioned is her aunt. My question is, can you think of a possible connection between what I saw and Piper's disappearance?"

"Well, the only thing I can think of right now is that she might have gone to see her mother, but surely the police will already have been told everything there is to know about her family, and they will be looking into that possibility."

"Yes, that's what I thought too. I just didn't want to be holding back on anything that might help."

"Anyway, how would you explain knowing that? It's not like you can tell them the truth."

"True, but if you thought it was important, I guess I could lie and say she confided in me."

Before she gets off the bus, Sophie promises to call me if she thinks of anything else.

Over dinner, I tell Dad about Piper's disappearance. On the off chance that the police want to question me further, I mention that I saw her out the weekend before last, and that I shared this information with the detectives today. The story makes the local television news, and we watch it together. Toby's dad is interviewed, as is a woman described as Piper's aunt and legal guardian. She looks distraught, but manages not to cry as she pleads with the viewers for any information that will help the police to find Piper. Then the screen is filled with Piper's smiling face. It is her school photo, taken earlier this year.

"She's a pretty girl," Dad comments. "I hope they find her safe very soon."

The time is almost seven, and Rosie hasn't called. I wonder if the stress of last night is at all responsible for her deterioration today. I spend a few hours doing school-work, and hoping that Sophie might call with an idea, but she doesn't. I am in bed by eleven and asleep soon after.

# Chapter 35

I am no artist, but I have always enjoyed drawing, and this is no exception. The picture I am working on is a childish one, but I am not bothered. A straight line delineates the ground from the sky, with one large tree standing left of centre. 'V' shapes on the ground signify tufts of grass. A perfectly square house, a chimney jutting out from its slanted roof, sits to the right. Wisps of smoke curl upwards in a spiral out of the chimney's opening. The sun is perfectly round, with swirly yellow and orange rays curling out of it, all the way round. The sky has three identical, fluffy clouds suspended in it, and four birds are depicted by 'm' shapes, flying in the sky. As I colour the grass green, one of the birds begins to float out of the sky. It lands delicately on a V-shaped blade of grass, forming a perfect heart.

My heart is pounding, and I am sitting bolt upright in bed, covered in a sheen of sweat. I have to call Toby, but as I get out of bed I notice the clock. It's 5:19 am, far too early to call anyone, but I have to do something. I get up, shower, dress and write a note for Dad, telling him that there is nothing to worry about, but I had to leave early. I don't lie, but I don't explain either. I mentally thank Mum for not letting me get a mobile phone. It makes times like these much easier. It is just after six when I eventually leave the house, so I decide to walk to Toby's. It will give me a chance to think about what I am going to say, as well as making me feel like I'm doing something. I honestly can't think of anything I want to do less right now than sit still.

It is 6:45 when I get to Toby's. If he isn't awake now, he will have to be soon. I walk round the side of his house, looking for a bedroom window. The first window I peer through clearly belongs to a living room; the second one, a kitchen. The third one is smaller with a blind drawn shut. Hoping this is Toby's bedroom, and not his father's, I tap on the window, gently at first, then with more gusto. The blind lifts revealing Toby's sleepy face. His look of surprise is almost comical, but what I have to say is so serious that I am unable to smile. He inclines his head to the right, indicating for me to go to the front door. He gets there before I do, and walks towards me in the crisp morning air.

"Juno, what is it? What's wrong?"

I have had plenty of time to prepare this speech, but somehow I can't seem to get the words out.

"Come inside where it's warm."

His arm is around me as he guides me through the front door, and into the same sitting room I looked into only minutes ago. A framed photo of Toby and his parents sits on a mantlepiece above a fireplace. Something about the sight of this picture kickstarts my brain into action.

"Toby, you have to listen to me, and you have to believe me!" I say pleadingly.

"Of course, what is it?"

"Before I start, you have to promise to accept what I'm going to tell you is the truth."

"Ok, I promise," he says solemnly.

"The vision I had when I touched that horrible man in the surgery. The naked woman tied up. It was Piper!"

"How can that be? I thought you said it was his girlfriend, the nurse."

"I know what I said, but I was confused because they both have red hair. I didn't get to see her face, but I did see a small tattoo on the back of her neck, and Piper has one of those too."

"Juno, these days, tattoos are incredibly common."

The look on my face registers my frustration. "What sort of tattoo did you see?"

"It was an outline of a heart."

Although I didn't actually see a heart, I know with absolute certainty that that's what I would have seen if her hair hadn't been covering the top half of it.

"You're totally sure about this?"

"Toby, you promised." He's probably regretting that now, but he is careful not to show it.

"Sorry. Ok, we need to speak to Dad. He didn't come home last night so we'd better get to the station as I really don't think this is something we can do over the phone."

I am in total agreement, so while Toby quickly dresses, I call for a cab.

On arrival at the police station, Toby speaks to the desk sergeant, explaining who he is and that he urgently needs to see his father. This really isn't the way I'd imagined meeting Toby's father, but that can't be helped. We are ushered through a door and asked to wait. The space we are in is open-plan, with about a dozen desks scattered around. Roughly half of them are occupied, and most of the occupants are on the phone. On a huge whiteboard is a blown-up image of Piper, the same one shown on the television news last night. There are four arrows drawn from the base of the photo, each leading in different directions. I spot my name in amongst the writing at the end of one arrow.

The desk sergeant returns, gesturing for us to follow him. He leads us down the centre of the room to a door set into a glass wall bearing the sign *Inspector Moxham*. Toby's father looks harried and not at all pleased to see us. However, as Toby introduces me, he seems to soften slightly at the mention of my name.

"Dad, I need you to listen very carefully to what I'm going to tell you. You are going to have to trust that what I'm telling you is the truth, no matter how crazy it sounds."

"Toby," he says impatiently. "I honestly don't have time for this right now. As you are well aware, a young girl is missing, and you of all people shouldn't have to be told that at this crucial stage in the investigation, *every* minute counts."

"This is about Piper, Dad. Trust me, you are going to want to hear this."

"Go ahead then, but please make it quick," he says as he dismisses the desk sergeant. Before speaking again, Toby reaches for my hand, taking it into both of his.

"I told you about what happened to Juno's mum, right?"

"Yes," he says before turning to me with a look that is simultaneously apologetic and sympathetic.

"Juno, I'm terribly sorry for your loss."

I acknowledge this with a small smile, still petrified at the thought of how he is going to react to what he is about to hear.

"And I mentioned Juno's illness after her mum's accident?"

"Yes, you did."

"Ok, now this next piece of information will be hard to take in, but you need to trust that everything I say is the absolute truth."

Toby's dad is already looking bewildered, and he hasn't heard anything yet.

"Ok, Toby, but please get to the point."

"When Juno regained consciousness in the hospital, she found that she could read people's recent memories just by touching them."

Immediately, Inspector Moxham's face is one of disbelief. He isn't even trying to conceal his incredulity.

"Dad, I found it hard to believe too, but I can guarantee that Juno really has an ability to read memories."

"Well, perhaps she does, but I fail to see what any of this has to do with Piper's disappearance."

"Dad, Juno knows who has Piper!"

"What? How? You've lost me."

"Juno works in a medical practice and sometimes has to take a patient's blood pressure. On Saturday, the day after Piper went missing, a man came into the surgery, and Juno had to take his blood pressure. When she touched him, she saw a red-haired woman naked and tied face down to a bed."

"No disrespect, Juno, but even if I accept that you have this ability, a redhead face down on a bed could be anybody."

For the first time since we entered the room, I speak. "I saw a heart tattoo on the back of her neck."

At this, I detect a brief flicker of interest in his eyes. So I was right. Even though I was certain before, I am pleased to have it confirmed. Sadly, the spark is gone again as quick as it came, and is replaced by its predecessor, a look of doubt and disbelief.

"Juno, please understand that this is in no way intended as a slight, but you go to school with the girl, you have seen her tattoo before, you know she is missing, you are going through a very emotional time in your life - it was probably a form of dream. It certainly isn't enough for me to get me a search warrant, let alone make an arrest."

"Dad, Juno had the vision before we heard Piper was missing."

This simply has no effect whatsoever. I realise now that no amount of talking is going to work. Nothing Toby or I say is going to convince him of the truth. I am also aware that Piper's life is at stake, so I do the only thing I know how to. Opening the door, I walk back into the main workspace. The closest desk to me is occupied by a female constable, identified by a nameplate on her desk as Constable Emma Sheller. I ask her if she wouldn't mind coming into the Inspector's office for a moment. Her look is one of confusion, but I see curiosity there too, so she obligingly stands and follows me back into the office.

"What's going on here?" asks Inspector Moxham.

"Dad, please just give Juno a chance to show you why you need to believe her."

Sitting down, I ask the young woman if she would please give me her hand. She looks inquiringly at her superior, who nods and shrugs as if to say, let's just get this over with. Briefly I worry that the only time I am desperate to have a vision, perhaps there will be no memory to read. As she tentatively extends her hand towards me, I take hold of it...

And find myself in a green-tiled, Art-Deco bathroom, with a huge, claw-foot tub and large bevelled mirror on the wall. There is a wooden shelving unit, holding two green bottles and two navy towels, as well as an assortment of products for both men and women. In my hand, I am holding a white plastic stick with a small window in it. In this window, two vertical pink lines are visible...

I gently let go of her hand, and after thanking her, I turn to Toby's dad. I describe the Constable's bathroom in detail, from the tiles to the colour of the towels, even naming some of the products on the shelves. Constable Sheller is impressed, but Toby's dad is unmoved.

I was hoping that would be enough, but it seems I have no choice. Looking to the constable I apologise, before adding, "She's pregnant." One look at her face is all it takes to confirm that this is correct. "How could you possibly know that? I only took a test three days ago?" She turns to look at me, with a mixture of awe and confusion. Thankfully, even Toby's dad seems to be taking me seriously now.

Within minutes, I am in an interview room with the same two detectives I spoke with at school. I give them details of the scene I witnessed on Saturday when I took Zachary Sharp's blood pressure. The only detail I alter slightly is the description of the tattoo. They keep their disbelief in check, but it is clear that they are sceptical. At this point, I care little for what they, or anyone else thinks; I just want Piper to be found. The interview takes around forty-five minutes, after which Toby's dad asks a male constable to drive us back to his home, where he asks us to wait until we hear from him.

Hours later, when the phone rings, Toby answers it, listens briefly and then passes the phone to me.

"Hello?"

"Juno, I wanted you to know that we found Piper in Zachary Sharp's apartment. She was drugged, dehydrated and barely conscious but the doctors assure us that she will make a full recovery. We have you to thank for that."

# Chapter 36

## Two months later

I wake to the sound of my alarm and for a few moments I am uncertain what day it is. As the knowledge that it is Saturday slowly settles into me, I roll on my side to look at the photo of the three of us. I find myself wishing that I could remember more about that day, more about many days. If only the Gift worked with photographs of people and not just the people themselves.

I have spent a lot of time thinking about the Gift and the fact that it is something Mum and I shared. Despite the fact that she isn't alive and that when she was neither of us were aware that the other bore the burden, I still feel it has somehow strengthened the bond between us and continues to do so. Rosie continues to be my saviour although I fear her illness is getting worse.

Dad drops me at the surgery on his way to the supermarket. The waiting room is empty. I never fail to think of Zachary Sharp when I walk into the reception area, which inevitably leads to thoughts of Piper. Although it was my decision to keep my involvement in the case a secret, some small part of me wishes Piper knew I had something to do with her being rescued. I guess that's just vanity but the fact is I feel like we have been through something enormous together and she has absolutely no idea.

Piper missed almost a month of school. Watching everyone react when she reappeared on her first day back brought up painful memories of my return after Mum's accident. People stopped, stared, whispered and pointed, avoiding her yet at the same time drawn to her as though she was some rare and potentially dangerous animal on display. None of them gave any thought at all as to how it might make her feel. Unlike me, Piper doesn't even have the safety net of a friendship group to shield her. I tried to act as normally as possible, not wanting to add to her troubles, but I too was as curious, if not more so, than everyone else.

Outwardly, although she seems not to have changed at all there is something almost imperceptibly different about her. Before, she seemed totally self-contained, proud, majestic even. Since she came back, although she still keeps to herself, she seems softer somehow, more vulnerable. I don't know if this change is noticeable to others or if it is even real. Perhaps it is all in my imagination.

My reverie is interrupted by Sue's arrival. Enthusiastically, she gives me a recap of what has gone on in her life in the fortnight since I saw her last. There seems to be no end to the parties and gatherings she attends. I marvel at how different her life is from mine.

Before long, patients start arriving and we are both kept busy for a few hours. The flow of patients slows as the morning wears on and there is only one woman for me to attend to while Sue takes her break. Before taking her into the nurse's room, I check her name in the appointment book. She is listed as Kate Webb. She is a very slim, pretty woman, who clearly takes care of herself. She is friendly and chatty, asking me about the school I attend whilst I weigh her. I am careful to sit down before taking her blood pressure.

I have very few visions these days as I generally touch the same people day in and day out. Now that people aren't expressing their condolences anymore, there is a lot less touching going on. My Saturdays in the surgery are sometimes the only visions I have all week. The patient is talking about her daughter Megan. I mentally prepare myself as I place my fingers on the inside of her wrist to measure her pulse…

I am sitting at a granite-topped kitchen bench, sipping tea and flicking through a magazine, when the iPhone on the counter next to me rings. The name on the phone says Dr. Richmond. I answer the phone before the second ring sounds.

"Dr. Richmond? Do you have my results?"

Although I can't feel it, I can hear the anxiety in her breathless speech. A voice I am very familiar with answers.

"Yes, Katie, and you will be happy to hear that they are totally clear. There is nothing to worry about. I would like you to come back in just to discuss where we go next, but now that we have crossed anything nasty off the list, you can relax."

This she does, even without the emotion present, I can sense every cell in her body uncoil…

Toby is waiting for me in the street as I emerge just after three o'clock. He tells me about the rugby match and I tell him about the vision I had. I never give him names, but it is nice to be able to share the things I see. Even though the majority have nothing to do with me, they each leave their mark.

It is cold and the sky threatens rain, so we decide to go indoors. We find a café, and sit at a table for two by a large bay window. At the table next to us, a man and a woman are having an animated discussion about something. I immediately recognise her as the pregnant female constable, Emma someone, her last name escapes me now. She is one of the few people who are aware of my Gift. Along with the two detectives who interviewed me, Inspector Moxham apparently swore her to secrecy and she seems to have been true to her word.

Emma glances over at Toby as we sit, and I watch as realisation dawns on her. She smiles openly at Toby before turning her eyes to me. The only word to describe her reaction to seeing me is dread, bordering on revulsion. She is clearly so uncomfortable being near me that within minutes she has convinced her companion they need to leave. Perhaps they were ready to go anyway, but even as I am trying to persuade myself of this, the thought of the look I saw on her face only moments ago tells me otherwise. Glancing at her stomach as she stands, I can see a small bulge that I imagine to most would go totally unnoticed.

If nothing else, this encounter reassures me that I made the right decision to keep the Gift a secret from everyone but Rosie, Sophie and Toby. Despite the fact that she knows that, as a result of the Gift, I was able to help solve a case and potentially save someone's life, Constable Emma still reacted to me as though I was a pariah. Toby senses my unease and does his best to stop me from taking it personally.

"You can't blame her. From her point of view you're the girl who dragged her into her boss's office, touched her hand, and then, out of nowhere, described her bathroom in intricate detail, before disclosing the fact she was pregnant, just days after she found out herself. Let's face it, it's not your average daily encounter. To her, you must seem like something out of a Stephen King novel."

He is totally right, and I am only pleased that there are very few people out there, who will see me in the same light. The episode has done away with my appetite so I only order a juice. Toby orders a BLT with the works. His appetite is something that never ceases to astound me. When his meal arrives, his obvious enjoyment of it is contagious and consequently my mood improves.

By the time we leave the café, a major storm is underway. Huddled closely together, we duck under shop awnings in a vain attempt to keep dry, as we make our way to the nearest bus stop.

Once back at my place, we spend a lazy evening watching television with Dad. The clock shows 6:42 when I glance at it. I realise that I am becoming so used to nights without a call from Rosie that I often forget to check the time. The grip her illness has on her now seems stronger. Tomorrow's visit is bound to be a fruitless one. Despite this, and even with the glaringly empty space on the sofa where Mum used to sit, I feel a sense of peace that only three months ago I would not have imagined possible.

# Chapter 37

## Six months later

I am lying on my back, staring up at a blue, cloudless sky. Beneath me is a bed of grass so soft it feels like velvet. There are tiny white flowers dotted around, each centre a drop of liquid gold gleaming in the sunlight. Someone is holding my hand. When I incline my head slightly to the right, I see Mum's beautiful face in profile. She has her eyes closed. Her skin is so clear I can see the blue-green veins near her temple. Wearing a long white dress, her feet bare and her hair fanned out around her like a halo, she looks like a celestial being. Our fingers are entwined, our hands fitting perfectly together like adjacent pieces in a puzzle. She opens her eyes and turns her blue-eyed gaze to meet mine. She smiles her incredible smile and it is as though someone has turned up the intensity of the sun's rays. The warmth suffuses my whole being. I could happily lie like this forever.

I open my eyes and the very same glorious smile greets me. A feeling I haven't experienced in a long time comes over me. I lie with it for a while - not questioning or judging it, just savouring it. I soon realise the sensation is one of contentment. The void left by Mum's death will never be filled but it is no longer a cavernous pit waiting to swallow me whole. The chasm is still there but I have learnt to skirt around it. I have even begun to build a bridge over it so that I can imagine at some future time being able to cross it safely without fear of falling in.

There are still times when heartache threatens to overcome me but it doesn't happen as often as it used to, and I am getting far better at dealing with it when it does. Sylvia helped me understand that resisting negative feelings only strengthens them, giving them ever-greater power. Instead, I have learned to sit with the sadness when it comes, accepting it, and letting it go when it is ready.

Although we don't see Sylvia anymore, the things she taught me were invaluable. Not only in dealing with my grief over Mum but also in managing my feelings about Rosie's illness. The last six months have seen Rosie's spates of bad days gradually lengthen so that her worst streak was one of thirteen days just last month. The average run has grown. It used to be common for her to disappear into herself for four or five days. Now, when the bad days start, we are lucky if she comes back to us after eight or nine days. On the plus side, her good days still often come in threes and we continue to be grateful for them. The doctors are fairly certain that her deterioration is due to Mum's death. Although the doctors have made changes to her treatment to try and halt her decline, they don't seem to be very effective.

I am in no hurry this morning as I have taken a rare day off work so as not to miss Teya and Eliot's fifth birthday party, which starts at midday. I go to the kitchen and find Dad standing at the stove, whistling along with the music and flipping a pancake high into the air, before catching it smoothly. He must be hungry as there is a small pile already stacked on a plate next to him. Just smelling them whets my appetite too and I prepare the condiments, slicing a lemon for me and a banana for him and placing them along with the maple syrup onto the breakfast counter. Between mouthfuls of pancakes, I fill Dad in on what Sophie told me last night. Some child in the playground pushed Teya off a see-saw and while an X-ray ruled out a break, she sprained her ankle quite badly. Annie was considering cancelling the party but decided that to re-schedule would be too difficult.

Dad and I are collecting Toby at eleven so we can all go shopping together for the twins' birthday gifts. Toby is waiting outside his house when we arrive and before long we are at the shopping mall. Dad and Toby are talking cricket as we make our way to the toy store. Although I have no interest in the game whatsoever, seeing the two of them talking so easily together adds to my feeling of happiness.

Once inside, we all agree that buying the twins one thing that they can both use is the way to go, so we begin in the games section. Finding a game that is suitable for five year olds and will interest both boys and girls is easier said than done. Dad and I scour the shelves together, considering and discounting game after game, until Toby calls us over to the sports section.

"I had one of these when I was a kid," he says pointing to a totem tennis set. "They're great fun and you can play on your own or against someone else."

Dad and I agree that it's a perfect present and the woman behind the counter kindly offers to wrap it for us.

Balloons adorn the eucalyptus tree on the corner of Sophie's street and a sign in the shape of an arrow attached to a lamp post reads *Twins' Party This Way*. The weather is absolutely perfect so instead of going to the front door, we walk round the side of the house, heading straight for the back garden. It is only minutes after midday but the garden seems to be full of children already. Eliot is jumping on the trampoline with two other boys while another group of children are chasing each other around it. Perhaps because the sound of so many small children is one I so rarely hear, I really notice it now.

Sophie walks out of the back door, balancing a huge tray of sausage rolls on one arm and a platter of fairy bread on the other. "Hi guys," she calls, smiling happily at us as she moves to put the food on a table set up under an awning. She relieves Toby of the bulky box calling to Eliot to come and accept the gift. He waves distractedly from the trampoline and calls out a 'hello' in our general direction but clearly has no intention of doing anything more than that. More guests are arriving behind us and Sophie greets them as we move deeper into the garden.

Moments later, Annie appears with Teya perched on her hip, her sore foot in a gauze bandage which, by the looks of it, is more to remind people about her injury than to provide any source of support. Annie sees us and immediately comes over. She greets us all with kisses and asks Teya to do the same. She is sulking and buries her face in Annie's neck and I am reminded of one of Mum's favourite songs, *It's My Party and I'll Cry if I Want To*, which makes me smile. Annie tells Dad there is someone she wants him to meet and begins to guide him across the garden.

Halfway across, she deftly passes Teya to Sophie who is making her way back to us. She is nuzzling Teya's neck and making her giggle and when she comes to a stop in front of us, Teya reaches her arm out towards me. Sophie and Toby both look at me questioningly but I can hardly disappoint the birthday girl, so I take Teya into my arms...

I am sitting on a see-saw in a playground with children everywhere. There is a dark-haired girl sitting opposite me and as my seat nears the ground, I bend my knees and push my tiny feet into the ground beneath me, giving myself maximum leverage for the upswing.

"Get off, Teya, it's my turn!" A fair-haired boy in a green t-shirt is yelling.

"But I just got on!" retorts Teya, not unkindly. As my end of the see-saw is about to start its next upward trajectory, the boy moves towards me with one arm outstretched. Without thinking, I react and watch as Teya's small arm shoots out to fend off the green-shirted boy. I remain seated on the see-saw as the fair-haired boy falls backwards into the dirt, winded yet otherwise unhurt. The see-saw continues to rise and fall with me seated on it, as the blonde boy, crying now, picks himself up and runs off in the direction of a group of mothers…

I am back in Sophie's garden with Teya still in my arms. I am not sure what just happened. Never before have I been able to have any influence over the action in a vision. By now Teya has begun wriggling to be released. Toby and Sophie have their backs to us and are deep in conversation with some other party guests. Unsure as to what just happened, I gingerly place Teya on the ground and watch, astounded, as she literally bounds off on two very able legs. Neither Toby nor Sophie is taking any notice of what just happened. Bizarrely, neither is anyone else. Strangest of all, the bandage that was definitely around her ankle before, is nowhere to be seen. It's as if her accident never happened at all.

# Acknowledgements

Thank you to my mother Jacqui Wade for my love of reading.

Thank you to Louise King for your encouragement and support.

Thank you to Celine Faulkner for your inspiration & mentoring.

Thank you to Anoushka Weiley for your much valued advice.

Thank you to my son Jesse Harrington for being my first reader.

Thank you, Kelly Beaumont for bringing my cover design to life.

Huge thanks to Adele Brunner for so generously giving your time, energy & editorial expertise. You went above & beyond.

Special thanks to Chloe Harrington for reading for me after completing her IB.

Thank you to my family for putting up with me throughout this process.

*Touch & Tell* would not exist were it not for you all.

# About the Author

Samantha Harrington was born in 1968 in Sydney, Australia, where she was raised. She earned a BA from the University of Sydney in 1989. She worked in real estate in Sydney eventually co owning and operating a real estate business for ten years before moving with her husband and four children to Hong Kong in 2006, where she currently lives. This is her first novel.